The Me.. ...
Grey Suits

*Thought you knew how Princess
Diana died? Think again!*

A novel by L. P. Gibbs

depiction of London's Soho and the nefarious dealings that go on there.

Some of the events actually happened, some did not whilst others have been embellished to provide a more interesting story-line. I leave it to you to decide which is which.

* * * *

THE LAST PAYBACK.

Alan Randall had once been an enforcer for a minor gangster in London's Soho district. He was no stranger to death. Now in his late 60's, he had retired completely and lived quietly on the Kentish coast with his wife. That is, until a face from his past took him back on to a dangerous path of righteous vengeance and treachery as well.

There were many who had evaded the law but they could not escape the ultimate justice. There was the joy-riding child killer, a drugs baron, the Albanian people smuggler to name but a few, all of whom were deserving of his deadly interest. Randall succeeded where the legal system had let down the families of their victims.

BETHNAL GREEN, LONDON

24TH. SEPTEMBER 1997

The bullet hit the aged, yellowing brickwork mere inches above the fleeing man's head, showering him with a sprinkling of fine dust as he ducked into the alleyway that ran behind a row of shops in the parallel main road. The alley stretched out for more than two hundred yards before him and he knew he would not make it to the far end before they entered the alley behind him. With the street lights of the road at the end, he would be an easy target, silhouetted against the brightness. There was only one thing for it. He made an instant decision that was to ultimately save his life. To his right, a black metal drainpipe rose up into the darkness to a gutter at the top of a derelict factory. When pursuing a quarry, hardly anyone ever looked up, was his train of thought. He jumped up and got a good grip on the pipe, shimmying his way up at a rapid pace. This was no difficulty for him as it was his chosen trade. Within seconds, he was almost at the top, when the two men chasing him came round the corner at a run. He hugged the drainpipe and pressed himself against the wall, hardly daring to breathe. They stopped almost beneath him and he could hear their voices clearly drifting up from below.

"Where the fuck is he, Paul?" said the taller of the two. He was the one with a gun in his hand.

"Christ knows. He's got to be down here somewhere," his companion offered, speaking in lower voice. "He wouldn't have got to the end this quickly so he must be in one of the back yards. You start here and I'll go to the far end and we'll work towards each other." He ran off towards the end and started making his way back, vigorously searching behind the low brick walls into all the yards. His companion checked his pistol and began looking over the walls at his end. After six or seven minutes, he was fifty yards or so along the alley.

It was then that the man on the drainpipe felt a slight vibration shudder through the pipe. Looking up, a tiny trickle of dust fell upon him which told him that the rusting iron bracket was beginning to come loose from the wall. It wasn't used to holding that much weight. One way or another, it was time to move. After a quick glance down, he decided that was not the best course of action so he began to pull his way carefully further up the pipe and hooked his arm over the edge. A few moments later, following another couple of heart-stopping vibrations, his head was level with the guttering at the top. Cautiously, he peered over the edge and found a flat roof, some puddles of rain water glistening in the pale moonlight. He reached over and pulled himself over the parapet. As he did so, the ancient ironwork of the pipe finally gave way and clattered noisily to the ground way below him. He heard a shout from one of the pursuers and, looking back down, saw them running towards the falling pipe. The taller man raised his arm and almost immediately he heard the dull thud of the silenced handgun as two shots were fired off in quick succession. Throwing himself down on to the rooftop, he heard the whistling sound as the bullets flew past him and he could swear they were so close that he could feel the whisper of wind as they went by, harmlessly into the night air. He scrambled on all fours away from the edge then picked himself up and started to run to the far side of the roof, kicking up spray from the pools of water as he went.

When he reached the other side, there was a gap of around ten feet to the roof of the next building which was slightly lower. There came a shout from below and he saw one of the men pointing up towards him as he peered over the edge of the roof. The man on the ground kicked against a door and entered the factory. It wouldn't take him too long to reach the top floor. There was only one thing for it. He took half a dozen steps back, breathed in very deeply and started to run as fast as he possibly could. It was one of those snap decisions that people make when under extreme pressure. As he leaped across the ravine, he could not have known that the second man had seen him make the jump and had called to his colleague to follow him. The fugitive landed badly on the adjacent roof, twisting his left ankle and falling into a heap in another cold puddle. In the centre of the roof was a small, brick building with a wooden door set into it. He hobbled to it as quickly as he was able and tugged fiercely at the door. With no small effort, he managed to get it open and almost fell headlong down the the flight of metal steps inside. He recovered his balance and, dragging his left foot, went down two flights of stairs before he heard sounds below coming in his direction. There were two doors off the corridor by the staircase on this floor, both locked. To try to force one open would alert them to his location. A barred window was at the far end of the corridor with a bright street light immediately outside, shining through and lighting up the corridor. Limping painfully towards it, he laid down flat on the floor beneath the window and silently prayed to whichever God may be listening that the deep shadow he was laying in would suffice. Just seconds later, through the gloom he saw the two men arrive at the other end of the corridor from the staircase. Both were now brandishing guns. They stopped momentarily and glanced in his direction. If they couldn't see him, surely they would hear his beating heart pounding within his chest, he thought as he lay sweating, prostrate on the floor. Then, as his prayers were answered, the two men tried the two doors and ran up to the next floor. The fugitive slowly got to his feet and made his way gingerly down the stairs as he could hear them rummaging through rooms above. He emerged into the passageway he had leaped across only a few minutes earlier. Turning to his right, he came out on to Bethnal Green Road. Although it was after three in the morning, there were quite a few people around, Friday night revellers leaving the clubs. Feeling a little safer with others around him, he moved away as quickly as he could with his injury. Three hundred yards along the road he came across a minicab office, not much more than a hole in the wall and stumbled in through the door.

"Where you goin'?" asked the West Indian girl behind the heavy iron bars that went from floor to ceiling for her protection from the drunks.

"London Bridge Station please, love," he replied, wincing a little from the pain in his now swelling ankle.

"Bout five minutes, 'kay?" she replied, returning her attention to her magazine, not bothering to find out if it was okay. She flicked over the pages with bright fluorescent yellow fingernails. One of the cab drivers was seated to one side noisily eating a doner kebab.

"Can't *he* take me straight away?" asked the man, nodding in the direction of the obese driver. "I'm in a bit of a rush."

"I gots ta eat, man," said the driver with a frown. The prospective passenger took out some banknotes and waved them towards the driver.

"I'll pay you treble to go right now," he said. The driver's kebab landed in the bin in the corner as he jumped up and made for the door, his passenger limping behind him with the girl's giggling ringing in his ears. The man fell gratefully in to the back of the old Ford Cortina and pulled the door shut as he lowered himself down into the seat as far as he could below window level. Only seven or eight minutes later they were pulling up at London Bridge Station and the man got out.

"The fare's seven quid, mate, but you said you'd give me treble, yeah?" said the grinning driver, a gold tooth flashing in his wide mouth as he leaned across the gear-stick towards the side window of the car. The passenger knew he was being ripped off but handed over a twenty pound note without a murmur, he was just glad to be well away from his pursuers. The minicab sped off with a screech of tyres, the rear end fish-tailing as it increased speed and the man walked slowly across the near empty forecourt to the taxi rank. He had decided on this course of action just in case enquiries were made at the minicab office and he wanted to put them off the scent if at all possible. There was only one cab on the rank, the driver reading a newspaper over half-moon glasses that perched on the end of his nose.

"Can you take me to Edmonton, pal?" the man asked. The cabbie made a show of sucking in his breath through pursed lips as he folded his newspaper and removed his glasses with a frown.

"It's a bit too far out for me, son," he responded, then smiled. "But I expect I *could* be persuaded to take you." The passenger drew another twenty pound note from his trouser pocket and handed it through the open window. It disappeared rapidly into the driver's leather money-bag. "You've persuaded me, get y'self in," he said with a grin and started the engine.

The journey took a little over twenty minutes at that time of the morning with little traffic and the man asked to be let off opposite Edmonton Town Hall, just before the roundabout. He waited for the taxi to make a U-turn and head back towards Central London before moving off. He turned into a little side street, passed a snooker hall and went under the railway bridge, coming out by some council flats, tower blocks that stood twenty stories high, the tops shrouded in mist. He continued straight ahead, checking over his shoulder from time to time to ensure he was not being followed. Entering Northern Avenue he felt sure he was safe and began to relax a little as he hobbled along. He did not know that eyes were watching him.

An old rusting, dirty, dark blue Transit van was parked halfway along the road, the wording 'R&J Builders' in faded cream lettering emblazoned along the side. The man who was sitting in the back of the van on a wooden crate with a cushion on it put down his cheese and pickle sandwich and focused his binoculars through the opaque rear window onto the approaching figure. Having confirmed that this was his target, he picked up his coded mobile phone and punched a pre-set button. It was answered after just one soft, purring ring.

"Zulu here," murmured the low voice in his ear. Geoff Carter, the observer in the van, knew the voice well but had never met its owner, was never likely to. The upper echelons of the British Secret Services rarely met the leg men or field operatives. 'Zulu' was no exception. The deep, slow talking voice only ever communicated through scrambled and coded telephones.

"Carter reporting, Sir. Our subject is approaching the house in Edmonton."

"Very well," said Zulu. "A back-up team will be sent. Keep observation and follow if he leaves before they get there."

"Understood," Carter replied, barely concealing a sigh. He was tired and had been cramped up in the back of the old van for over five hours. The two litre plastic bottle he kept solely for the purpose was just about full with his urine. Too many pints of lager before coming on duty, as well as the black coffee in his flask. The smell of stale sweat was beginning to get to him, along with the build up of flatulent gases that now permeated throughout the vehicle too.

The 'subject' kept looking behind him as he made his way slowly along the road. He eventually came to a dark green front door and tapped softly on the knocker. The pebble-dashed house was in complete darkness and showed no signs of life so he knocked again,

5

this time a little louder. A light came on in one of the upstairs bedroom windows and a woman's face appeared from behind a closed curtain as it was pulled to one side. She studied the man below for a few moments then made her way downstairs, muttering to herself. He heard the chain being gently taken off, then a bolt being slid across before the door opened.

"It's gone four in the sodding morning, Jimmy," she whispered with a scowl, turning up the collar of her gown against the cold of the early morning. "What do you want now? You'll wake the bleedin' kids up."

"Sorry, love," he told his sister, doing his best to look remorseful. "Got a bit of a problem and couldn't go back to my place."

"You've always got a bit of a problem, it seems to me," she said as she shuffled in her furry slippers towards the kitchen, stifling a huge yawn and tugging her dressing gown tighter around her ample waist. He followed her and slumped down on one of the hard, upright wooden chairs beside the table. The woman switched on the electric kettle, having shaken it to check that it contained enough water and took two white mugs down from the cupboard.

"What the hell have you done now?" she enquired with a sniff. "Who's after you? Is it the police again?"

"Don't go on, Trace, for Christ's sake," he replied, rubbing his forehead with a dirty hand. "First, I haven't done anything and second, it's not Old Bill I'm worried about. *They* wouldn't be such a bastard problem." He watched her go through the routine of spooning coffee and sugar into the mugs.

"So who is it this time?" she asked with a certain amount of indifference. She just wished her younger brother wouldn't always come to her house at the first sign of trouble. It had happened too often in the past and, in her heart, she knew it would always be that way. As usual, he was there again with his problems. She placed a mug of coffee on the table before him. He raised it to his lips without so much as a thank you. Once again, he was taking her for granted. She briefly thought about telling him to go, but couldn't do it. For all his faults, he had always helped her out whenever he had money, to the point of being extravagant. With her husband having gone on the missing list, yet again, she was always grateful for the help he always gave her whenever he had money and the children adored him, too.

"No-one for you to worry about," came the answer to her question. She shrugged and sipped at her own drink. "Just got a little problem to sort out at the moment and need somewhere to crash for a couple of days, is all. Got anything to eat, Trace?" he asked hopefully. "I'm bloody starving."

"You always are," she replied, turning back to the cupboard behind her. "I can do you a ham and pickle sandwich but that's about all I can spare. I've got two kids to feed, you know."

"That'll do, anything."

"What sort of problem have you got now then?" she enquired, not really caring about the answer she would receive. She knew that, as usual, she wouldn't get the truthful answer from him.

"The bloody questions you ask, Trace."

"Well, you've got a perfectly good flat of your own," she persisted. "Why can't you go back there?" He shook his head and wrinkled his nose as if it were a minor irritation that would eventually go away, although he knew it certainly would not. Things had gone way too far for that.

"Someone I owe is looking for me and they won't take no for an answer," he lied with absolute conviction. "I'll get hold of a bit of cash within a few days and sort it all out." Tracy yawned once again and set her empty coffee mug down on the stainless steel draining board of the sink, turned and folded her arms, looking down at her brother with a stern expression.

"You'd better, Jim," she told him sternly. "I don't want those kind of people coming here, looking for you and upsetting the kids. They're already upset about their dad pissing off again." He smiled reassuringly at her.

"I don't know why you bother with that wanker, Trace, honest I don't. Don't worry though," he said. "They don't know anything about you." He got up and limped through to the front room and flopped down on the settee. A few moments later, Tracy came in and threw a heavy blanket on his lap.

"Don't give me any grief, Jim. I mean it," she said and went out. He heard her trudging back up the stairs and the click of the catch on her bedroom door as she closed it. He sank back, kicked off his shoes and raised his legs up on the cushions. Pulling the blanket up to his chest, he lay back and rested his head on the arm of the settee, gratefully closing his eyes. The pain in his ankle returned and kept him from sleeping. Instead, he went over everything that had brought him to this sorry state. The start of it all seemed a lifetime ago.

* * * *

PIMLICO, LONDON

FEBRUARY 8th 1997

James Arthur Hogg was born to a working class family in Durants Road, Ponders End, a suburb of Enfield in North London in 1949. He had a long, angular face and his father always insisted on plastering his unruly hair down with Brylcreem. This was somewhat unfortunate for young James as he also had protruding ears and the sleeked back hair only accentuated this anomaly. Due to his seemingly big ears, his school friends cruelly nick-named him Noddy throughout his junior school years. It wasn't until he was admitted to the George Spicer Central School in Enfield at the age of eleven that he started to become a rebel. His best friend at school was Alan Randall in whom he found a kindred spirit. Both lads hated most of the lessons, especially the hour long Chemistry lessons on Monday afternoons between three and four o'clock. They always sneaked out of school just before the sessions started. Getting away with it for so long, they graduated to truancy two or three times a month, spending their days in the parks when the weather was fine or nursing a single cup of coffee in the cafe on the corner of Aberdare Road opposite the bus garage if it was raining or cold. Then one day Alan was caught in a delicate situation with the Head Girl during the lunch break and expelled from school. This left James Hogg without a close friend or ally. His behaviour and school work deteriorated even more to the point where, at the age of fifteen, he was told that it would be pointless to return to school after the summer holiday. A polite way of telling him that he too was being expelled.

Hogg drifted from one dead-end, badly paid job to another, punctuated by long periods of unemployment. At times, he would meet his old school friend Alan and spend time in his company. Alan Randall was not a good influence on him and they got into a number of scrapes at times. Once, they invented a way of getting free cigarettes. One of them would buy a packet of twenty Embassy filter cigarettes. Then, using a thin knife, they would carefully open the cellophane at the top of the pack and gently slide the packet up until the top was clear of the cellophane. The pack was opened and the cigarettes removed to be replaced with one and a half pages of the Daily Mirror, exactly the same weight. Pack closed and slid back down, a heated knife blade slid across would re-seal the packet's cellophane once more. Alan was the braver of the two and he would enter a tobacconist shop asking for twenty Embassy. When the shop-keeper had placed the pack on the counter, Alan would then ask for a box of matches as well. When the shop-keeper turned round for the matches, Randall would quickly exchange the pack of cigarettes for the false pack in his pocket. He would then state with sadness that he had forgotten his wallet and leave. The fake pack was put back on the shelf. Sometimes they could go for several weeks without having to buy a pack. Then Alan found a job as a driver's mate for a haulage company and Hogg rarely saw him after that. Randall appeared to enjoy the work and offered to try to get him a job there as well but hard work was something to be avoided at all costs as far as Hogg was concerned.

He managed to get by with shop-lifting and stealing radios from unlocked cars but money was always tight. Seven years passed in this manner and it was inevitable that he mixed with the wrong type of company. With the aid of an acquaintance, he began his house-breaking career. Partly due to his skill but mainly good fortune, he found he was successful and decided to try working alone to avoid sharing the spoils. He developed a gift for climbing drainpipes and brickwork and was responsible for some of the more audacious burglaries in the Highgate and Hampstead areas of London where, being affluent districts, he found rich pickings. A few months later he was caught leaving a property with several thousand pounds worth of jewellery, arrested and spent three long months in Pentonville Prison.

The 'Ville', as it was known, was one of the oldest places of incarceration in London, opened in 1842 and built to hold just five hundred and twenty prisoners. It now held almost twelve hundred. From the centre hall, five wings radiated outwards so that warders could see along each wing from one point. The cells, measuring thirteen feet by seven had small windows set high in the outside wall and housed two and sometimes three prisoners. Each thick, metal cell door opened on to a landing. Communal, evil smelling latrines were situated halfway along these landings on each side. During the night, prisoners had to make use of their pots for toilet purposes and the morning 'slop-out' in the latrine recesses often brought fights and arguments as everyone pushed and shoved to relieve themselves having held it all in overnight for fear of stinking out their cells. Cockroaches were a common site in all the cells and, in the enclosed exercise yard that was allowed to be used for just one hour a day, there was an infestation of rats. Huge, fat, scurrying brown things that flicked their tails as they scuttled along the edges of the walls to disappear through a hole once more. Hogg counted the days to his release. After that most unpleasant experience, he changed his method of working and moved his operations to the West End and Kensington areas.

It was in the West End of London that he renewed his acquaintance with Alan Randall, his old school friend. Randall was by then working as a heavy for Lenny Harris, a well known villain who operated a clip-joint in Great Windmill Street. Hogg bumped into him one night as he left a casino in Shaftesbury Avenue with a few pounds in winnings tucked into his pocket and went for a wander through Soho, hoping to find a working girl to keep him company for an hour or so. Randall was standing in the doorway of Silk's, the club run by Harris. He recognised Hogg immediately and called him across. They shared several drinks in a nearby illegal drinking house and chatted, catching up on deeds past. Hogg frequently saw him around the area after that.

Hogg would often go several months without making any money at all and then suddenly come across the perfect property for his skills. Whenever he made a big haul, he spent money like it was going out of fashion. New suits, casino visits, night-clubs, expensive restaurants and even more expensive women. He also made certain that his sister received money too. Even as children, she had always looked after him. It was never too long before his pockets were empty again. This was the life he led and, if he was honest with himself, the life he actually enjoyed. This life changed dramatically after the February of nineteen ninety seven.

For Hogg, the winter months were the hardest. Due to the inclement weather, most houses had their windows firmly closed and locked, making his job more difficult. On this particular wintry night however, he was in luck. He had parked his ancient Ford Sierra in Pimlico and, with turned up overcoat collar, was wandering the streets looking for any possibilities. He was beginning to feel a little desperate and had not had a touch since well before Christmas. As he walked along Charlwood Street, a well-dressed couple emerged from one of the large town-houses some hundred yards ahead of him. A Daimler Sovereign was parked in the kerb, the engine running and a chauffeur behind the wheel. The couple descended the eight steps to the pavement, got into the back and it purred gently away, blue-grey smoke curling from the twin exhausts. Hogg watched the car disappear round the corner at the end of the road and continued, slowing as he passed the house. To his amazement and delight, the bottom of a net curtain fluttered briefly in a second floor window. This meant that the sash window must have been inadvertently left slightly ajar. Hogg quickened his pace and went right around the block to his car. Climbing in, he removed his overcoat and rolled it up on to the back seat. He struggled into his black leather jacket, checking the inside pockets for his tools and pulled on his thin gloves. With his small rucksack over his left shoulder he set off, leaving his car unlocked in case of the need for a hasty getaway.

When he returned to Charlwood Street there was no sign of the Daimler and the house was still in complete darkness. With relative ease he climbed the drainpipe until he was next to the window with the fluttering curtain. He saw with glee that the window was indeed open barely an inch. It was enough. Hogg reached across and slid his gloved hand through the gap. Taking a deep breath, he swung his legs out and hooked one foot on to the window ledge. With his free hand he pushed the window up and pulled himself over the sill. He hung like that for a few moments with his legs dangling outside to listen for sounds from within and to allow his eyes to adjust to the darkness. There was just a small table with a plant on it in front of the window and, with his legs still outside, he gently lifted the table and moved it aside before carefully climbing in, pulling the window down to where he found it. He stood still and listened intently. There was no sound at all in the house. Making certain that the curtains were pulled together again behind him, he switched on his tiny pencil torch and surveyed the room he was in. It was a large bedroom with an enormous bed on one side, a walk-in type wardrobe, several chests of drawers and a huge, kidney shaped mahogany dressing table. It was with a fair degree of excitement that Hogg noticed a good sized jewellery box sitting on one side of the table. He lifted the lid gingerly in case it was one of those silly musical varieties that played something like Lara's Theme. It wasn't. The array of rings, bracelets and necklaces caused him to suck in his breath. What a result! The haul filled all of the zipper pockets in his jacket. He closed the lid again and a quick scout round the room told him that there was little else there to interest him. Moving silently to the door, he gripped the handle and put his ear to the panel. Still no sounds of life. Hogg opened the door and found himself on a polished wooden landing. Thick carpeted stairs led down and he took them slowly. He decided to pass the first floor and go to the ground floor before he made his way back up to his point of entry.

On reaching the entrance hall, he listened at the door to his left and, hearing nothing, gently opened the door. A quick flash round with his pencil torch showed he was in a man's study. There was a red leather topped desk, with a large window which faced the street and a high-backed leather chair behind it, a two seater sofa at an angle across one corner and two large, deep, comfortable looking armchairs. A bookcase stretched along the entire length of another wall. Heading for the desk, he stooped to the top drawer and then froze. He heard the front door opening and the sound of voices from the hallway. There was only one chance. Hogg threw himself over the small sofa in the corner and curled himself up into the smallest ball he could make of himself. The door to the study opened and he heard a man's voice.

"You two go on through to the lounge, my dear. Roger and I have to discuss some business." Hogg heard the door close once more and the sound of someone settling into the leather chair at the desk. There followed the clinking of glasses as drink was poured. "Damned shame the show was cancelled, old boy. We can order some food to be delivered later on." There was a brief pause before the man continued. "I was just wondering, what thoughts have you had on the confidential matter we were discussing last week,

Roger?" he heard.

"Well," came the reply, "we have come up with one possible idea but it would need some more work to perfect it. The remit that it must appear to be a tragic accident made it a little more difficult but I feel it may be feasible. It would obviously have to take place on foreign soil, preferably Paris where we can enlist the help of the French security services. They owe us a number of favours for things we have helped them with in the past, Algeria and all that. That way, if there ever was any implication of assassination, we could appear to be outraged at the dastardly act of a foreign power or terrorists." A lighter flared and the smell of cigar smoke filled the room.

"I would be interested to hear this plan of yours," came the first voice, slightly higher in tone.

"Due to the targets you have in mind, there will have to be witnesses to any accident, so this is what we propose." There came the sound of ice being dropped into a glass. "We intend to attach a small but quite powerful explosive device to a certain part of the steering mechanism of one of the cars that they frequently use. Our mechanical team will know exactly what section. The explosive would be detonated by remote control at exactly the right moment, causing the car to crash at a point where maximum damage would be achieved upon impact."

"I'm listening, go on."

"Should the main target survive the impact, we would ensure that the first ambulance on the scene would be one of ours, manned by two of our paramedics. They would ensure that neither of them ever reached the hospital alive. As both targets are always hounded everywhere by the paparazzi, there would be more than enough witnesses to the tragic accident and one of our chaps would be amongst them as pillion on a motorcycle to detonate the device." There was silence for a few moments as the first man obviously pondered over the proposition.

"Yeees," he said at length. "I can see that such a plan could very well work. Although the vehicle would obviously be thoroughly examined after the accident and traces of the explosives would be found. We can't have that, Roger."

"Of course, Andrew," replied Roger with confidence. "We had

14

taken that into consideration. With the aid of the French, we could substitute the damaged vehicle with another showing exactly the same damage. Our paparazzi photographer would help with his detailed photographs. Alternatively, arrange for the findings of any report to be changed in our favour. We could arrange for all the other photographers to have their cameras and equipment confiscated."

"And how do we know when they are likely to use this particular car?"

"We don't, I'm afraid. That is something we would have to leave to chance," came the reply. "As they often decide to change the car to be used at the last minute, sooner or later they *will* use the one we have rigged. It would be a Mercedes and we have a good relationship with quite a few high up executives within the Mercedes company so altering any findings should not be a problem. The couple we are looking at make frequent trips to Paris together so it should not be too long before the car is used."

"Excellent. I'll get the clearance from higher up, you understand, then hopefully we can start the ball rolling. I will get their visit dates for Paris and let you have them as soon as I get them. I must remind you, Roger, that this directive comes from the very highest authority and there must be no, I repeat *no* loose ends whatsoever. I'm sure you understand what I mean."

"That's perfectly understood, Andrew."

"Good. Can't have this damned woman marrying a Muslim, can we? Besides, all this kerfuffle that she's stirring up about those land-mines could seriously damage a lot of lucrative arms deals that are going on at the moment." There was a wheezing chuckle as the man known as Andrew rose noisily from his chair. "For the purposes of future reference, I think we should refer to this venture as Operation New Broom. What do you think of that, Roger?"

"New broom; sweeping clean? Sounds just right, Andrew."

"Well, we should rejoin the women in the lounge now, I think."

"Jolly good idea."

Hogg heard them go out of the study and the door softly closed behind them. He remained secreted in his hiding place for almost two hours before he heard the sound of goodbyes at the front door. The hall light that showed under the door went out as two sets of footsteps climbed the stairs. No time to hang around in case his intrusion into the bedroom was immediately discovered. Hogg crept to the front door. He found the key in the lock, gently slid off the chain and opened the door. The cold night air hit him like a brick wall, causing him to suck in his breath as he jumped down the steps. He tucked his head down and ran. When he reached his car just ninety seconds later, he threw his bag on to the passenger seat and started the engine. He made his getaway from the area keeping within the speed limits. Wouldn't do to get a tug from a prowling police car. As he drove into Hyde Park, he pulled in to the car park next to the Serpentine Cafe and parked, leaving the engine running to get the best from the weak heater. Unzipping his pockets, he emptied each one in turn and placed all the contents into his shoulder bag. If he should be captured, it would be easier to get rid of one small bag quickly rather than have to rummage through zipped pockets.

He then drove casually back to his small flat in Birkbeck Road, Tottenham, arriving shortly after one in the morning and carried his haul up the stairs, throwing it down on his bed. Sauntering in to the kitchen, he flicked down the switch on the kettle and spooned coffee into a mug. As he stood there waiting for the kettle to boil, leaning against the work-top, he pondered over the conversation he had overheard in Pimlico. Well-to-do people, he thought, yet planning some kind of assassination? Didn't seem possible. Still, what the upper classes got up to was none of his business. The kettle clicked off at boiling point and he poured the steaming water into the mug and added milk and sugar.

Back in the bedroom, he upended his bag and surveyed the contents spread before him. Plenty of gold there as well as numerous jewels. Bracelets, rings, necklaces, ear-rings, brooches, everything. He rummaged through his haul and decided to take it to Jewish Henry, a small time jeweller in Stepney. Hogg always got a reasonable price from Henry. He wasn't really Jewish but wore the traditional Hebrew skull-cap and sported the type of beard favoured in Stamford Hill Jewish society as he said it was good for business. By lunch-time of the following day, Hogg was five thousand pounds richer after his visit to Stepney.

* * * *

16

TOTTENHAM, LONDON

AUGUST 31st 1997

So it was that Jimmy Hogg continued his nefarious life without a thought for the eavesdropped conversation in Pimlico. Houses were burgled in the dead of night, stolen goods 'fenced' and the money quickly spent. That is until some six months later when, having had a recent good result with one of his break-ins, he had spent the previous night at The Golden Nugget Casino in Shaftesbury Avenue in the West End and flopped on to his little bed at three thirty five that morning after losing a considerable amount of money at the roulette table. He hauled himself out of the bed just after two in the afternoon and made himself a strong mug of coffee before going through to the front room and switching on the television. The date was Sunday, 31st August 1997 and the only image on the screen was a woman's photograph surrounded by thick, black edging. Diana, Princess of Wales was dead. The 'People's Princess' had been killed in an horrific car accident the night before in Paris. *Paris*?

Hogg banged his mug of coffee down on the table with a shaking hand. Paris! The memory of the hushed conversation he had overheard that night from behind a couch in the ground floor study of that house in Pimlico came vividly back to him. Surely not! It couldn't possibly be! Could it?

He sat there all afternoon and well into the evening, flicking between television channels, listening to all the reports that were coming in and taking in every detail of the news and information that was continually emerging from the crash scene. His head was swimming with data by midnight and he was now certain that what he had heard was the planning of the assassination of the Princess. Marry a Muslim, the man had said. Dodi Al Fayed? He was a Muslim, wasn't he? Diana had also campaigned against land-mines too, something else he had overheard. It was all beginning to fall into place now, making sense. He last remembered glancing at the clock at ten past three in the morning before drifting off to sleep in the armchair. At seven o'clock that morning he was wide awake, dressed, showered and had made the five minute walk to Lordship Lane to buy five different newspapers. Back at his flat with a coffee in front of him, he read everything. Of course, all the papers were full of the incident, running into dozens of pages complete with photographs and back stories.

Later that morning he went to Tottenham public library and searched all the back copies of the old newspapers for the two or three days after he had broken into the big house in Pimlico. After several hours of scanning and his head starting to spin, he found what he was looking for. A report in The Guardian that briefly mentioned in a single column a burglary at the Central London home of Lord Andrew Woolacott in Charlwood Street, Pimlico where seventeen thousand pounds worth of jewellery had been stolen. Seventeen fucking grand? That thieving bastard Henry had fiddled him once more! Either that or His Lordship had bumped up the insurance claim. The article went on to say that Lord Woolacott was a high-ranking civil servant working for the Government within the intelligence area in Whitehall. So, it *was* a British Government job after all! He walked back home mid-afternoon and gradually got through the best part of a bottle of Bushmills Irish Whiskey, trying to decide what he should do, if anything at all. After a short nap followed by a long shower, he ate a hastily assembled cheese and pickle sandwich and set off for the West End and Soho, the area he felt most at home in and where there were faces that he knew and trusted. He was seated in the window of Bar Italia, a coffee bar in Frith Street when a familiar face went sauntering by. It was Alan Randall. The man was now freelance and earning a living working for whoever paid him the most; enforcing, collecting and occasionally minding the door. Hogg tapped on the window and urgently beckoned him inside.

"Hello, Jimmy," Randall said, sitting down in the vacant chair opposite. "Haven't seen you for a while. Been busy?" Randall was always immaculately dressed in his customary black suit and tie and had the kind of eyes that were either as cold as ice or had a disarming smile behind them, depending on who he was looking at and what his intentions were. As he sat down, those steely blue eyes swiftly scanned the bar expertly, taking in the faces of everyone who was present and mentally noting them for future reference. He waved a hand in the general direction of the man behind the counter and within mere seconds a cup of coffee miraculously appeared before him on the table. Randall was well known.

"I could do with a chat, Al," Hogg replied in a whisper. "Might have got myself into something a bit hot." He went on to relate his tale; the break-in, the conversation he had overheard and what he had gleaned from newspaper articles and the television news programmes.

"Fuck me, Jim," Randall said, also in a whisper as he leaned across the table, glancing around to ensure they were not being overheard. "Sounds like you could be on to something, mate. From what you've told me, there's definitely some sort of connection there."

"Yeah, I know. Trouble is, what do I do about it? I can't go to the Old Bill for obvious reasons, can I? I feel like I should tell someone but I can't really trust anyone and I end up thinking that it might be best to just wipe my mouth and say nothing. What d'you reckon?" Randall appeared to ponder over the dilemma for a few moments before making his reply.

"What about the newspapers then? Just think how much wedge they would pay for a story like this. It'd probably run well into six figures. You could retire somewhere nice and warm, out of the country maybe. Once the paper printed it, you'd be safe, my son. They wouldn't dare come after you then."

"That's a thought," Hobbs responded, nodding slowly with a slight frown as he considered the idea. It was a possibility that he had not considered and may just help him. "I might do just that, Alan. I'll have a bit of a think about it and keep you posted." Randall got up, looked at his expensive gold wristwatch and slapped Hogg on the shoulder as he spoke.

"Well if you do go and draw a nice little earner from this, you'll need someone to look after you, won't you? You know where to find me, mate," he said with a smile. "Let me know how you get on, Jimmy and give me a bell if you need a hand. I'm looking for something different to get me out of all this crap in Soho and this could just be it if there's a few quid in it for me." Randall gave him a friendly wink, shuffled his way through the other customers, went out into the street and disappeared from view. Hogg looked in the direction he had gone and wondered if he had done the right thing by confiding in Alan Randall. They were old mates but that often counted for nothing where money was involved. Then again, Alan was a decent enough bloke and he also knew the right useful faces if needed. He was well known in Soho, recognised as one of the 'faces' to watch out for.

The following morning, Roger Whitehead entered Lord Woolacott's office, having been summoned five minutes earlier by telephone. He had been expecting to be called to the meeting all day and felt he was in a comfortable position to answer any of the old man's questions. Stopping outside the door, he straightened his tie before entering. It wouldn't do to enter the room with his tie askew. The old boy would always notice anything like that immediately.

"Ah, Roger," His Lordship sighed with a huge smile spread across his face. "Sit y'self down, my boy. Have a whisky, won't you? I've got a rather special single malt that I've been keeping for just such an occasion." Pouring two over-large measures of single malt scotch into cut-glass tumblers from the decanter behind his chair, Lord Woolacott, with the aid of a heavy, gold plated Ronson table lighter, lit one of his fat Havana Grade A cigars and exuded sheer happiness from every pore in his ample body. He offered one to Whitehead who politely declined. "From what I hear, everything went as well as we had hoped."

"It did, indeed, Andrew," Whitehead replied, sitting in the offered chair before the desk. "The gentleman died immediately following the impact and the other person, although sustaining near fatal injuries, received a lethal dose of morphine after being taken away in our ambulance which was following the pack of paparazzi. She was pronounced dead upon arrival at the hospital. The driver did not survive the impact either. There is the slight problem of the bodyguard who was in the front passenger seat but, at present, he recalls nothing of the accident. We shall have to see how he progresses. He is a practical man, by all accounts, so it may not be a problem. We may have to have a word with him at some stage, we'll see."

"A satisfactory outcome to the entire operation, I think. Any loose ends, so to speak?" Woolacott raised a bushy eyebrow, his whisky glass halted halfway on its journey to his lips.

"One or two. No more than we anticipated but they will be eliminated within days. Steps have already been taken to ensure that those loose ends will be tidied up, if you know what I mean?"

"Of course. Very well done, Roger, you and your team seem to have got the job done as required." His Lordship said, nodding his approval. "The powers that be will no doubt be very content with what has been achieved." They talked for a little over half an hour before Whitehead left for his own office.

Instead of getting out of the lift at his own floor, he continued down to the basement garage and went to his private car. He sat behind the wheel and took out a small recording device, switching it on as he carefully looked around to ensure he was alone. He knew from experience that his numbered parking slot was just out of sight of the many security cameras dotted around in the interior of the basement garage. His car was the only place he believed to be safe from eavesdropping. The luxury vehicle was electronically 'swept' by his own team for covert microphones on a daily basis. Even so, he still spoke into the device in a whisper, only just loud enough to be picked up on the delicate recorder, just in case. He started, as always, with the date and time and his current location and then continued to bring the details up to date.

"Just had a meeting with Woolacott. Seemed very pleased with our Paris operation as previously mentioned," he whispered. He went on to recount his conversation with the peer almost verbatim. Whitehead had been keeping these notes ever since Woolacott had approached him with the request to find a way of eliminating what he called 'that infernal woman'. It was his fall back if things got bad for him. He could always say that he was simply following orders from above. It was not for nothing that Roger Whitehead had joined MI5.

At Cambridge University he had studied psychology to degree level. His written thesis on the use of psychological questioning for the interrogation of suspected terrorist detainees brought him to the attention of the highly secretive Department Five. Discreet questions were then asked around the campus and his tutors about him and his family before he was finally approached by a local recruitment agent. They learned about his upbringing from his birth in East Anglia, all about his parents, grandparents and, of necessity, his extended family.

Whitehead had been an outstanding scholar at his local grammar school in Ipswich and his elevation to Cambridge was never in doubt. He also excelled in sporting events from football and cricket to tennis. A wiry, if slim individual, he was popular with the girls at school, always having one on his arm at the weekends and when attending the regular school dances.

* * * *

MERCEDES EUROPE TEST CENTRE

MUNICH, GERMANY

10th. SEPTEMBER 1997

The large, flat-bed truck rolled through the security guarded gates of the vehicle testing and examination centre on the huge industrial estate on the outskirts of Munich. The load on the back was covered with a heavy-duty, green tarpaulin and secured with padlocked chains. Ahead of the lorry were two police motorcycle outriders with their blue lights flashing. Another two brought up the rear. The motorcyclists stopped just outside the gates and the truck disappeared inside a cavernous warehouse, the massive metal doors sliding closed with a noisy clang behind it. The on-board crane and hoist began to lift the cargo from the back, swinging it through ninety degrees and then lowering it gently to the polished concrete floor. Two men in white jump-suits unlocked the chains and carefully pulled back the tarpaulin to reveal a badly damaged, black Mercedes saloon. The two men waited beside the car.

Ten minutes later, two official looking men in business suits entered the warehouse by a small door to one side. An armed guard stood outside this door, a Heckler and Koch machine gun hanging by a strap from his shoulder. The men approached the wreckage and split up, each one wandering around it, inspecting every aspect of it.

"You understand what has to be done with this vehicle, Herr Grindt?" asked one of the men.

"Indeed, Your Lordship," came the reply. Martin Grindt had been in charge of the testing facility for almost fifteen years and knew everything there was to know about the working of their vehicles. "My men have their instructions which will be closely followed and I shall personally oversee every detail. By the time we are finished there will be no trace of any explosives. I am hopeful that the work will be completed by morning." As he spoke, he noted that one of the men in white overalls was circling the wrecked car, photographing it from every conceivable angle including the interior.

"Very good," Lord Woolacott nodded, his face expressionless. He bent forward to look closer inside the rear of the damaged car where blood stains covered the leather back seats. The roof of the car had been removed by firemen during the rescue operation. "I shall be at my hotel awaiting your progress report," he continued. "I, in turn, have to report to others."

"I understand completely," Grindt responded with a slight bow of his balding head. The two men shook hands and Lord Woolacott went out through the guarded door, getting in to his own chauffeur driven Mercedes waiting there. On arrival at the Charles Hotel situated on Sophienstrasse some fifteen minutes later, Woolacott picked up his mobile and hit a button.

"Zulu," came the voice when the call was answered.

"Hello, Roger," Woolacott said in his friendliest manner. "Everything is going as planned here, just thought I'd let you know."

"Good. I must confess that I was a little concerned about the journey from Paris to Munich. You never know how things will pan out in a foreign country. Paparazzi have a habit of getting information."

"Of course, but we followed the load all the way. French police escorted us to the border and then the Germans took over until we reached the test centre. Grindt knows what is expected of him and his team. Steps have been taken to ensure that everything is kept under wraps."

"I most certainly do feel a trifle easier now that the cargo has arrived at the site and the work can be done."

"Yes, me too, but it's here now and the report shouldn't take more than a few days, I am reliably informed." He drew in smoke from his fat cigar and blew it contentedly into a halo that floated up to eventually mushroom out like a miniature atomic explosion as it met with the high ceiling of his superior hotel room. "Once I've had eyes on the report, I'll fly back to Paris, see a couple of officials. I shall need to speak personally with the French senior pathologist also."

"Yes, of course."

"Right then, I think I'll potter down to the restaurant for dinner, old chap," he continued. "All that travelling on these bloody awful foreign roads has made me quite ravenous."

"I'll let you get on with it then," Whitehead replied with a faint smile and switched off his phone. He sat back in his chair at MI5 Headquarters and clasped his hands behind his neck, deep in thought. The sooner this was all over the better he would feel. If only they could sort out this infernal business with that bloody cat-burglar.

Over in Munich, Lord Woolacott, replete from his chateaubriand meal, settled into the super king-sized bed and quickly nodded off without a care in the world. He awoke at six thirty the following morning as he always did without the need for an alarm. By eight thirty he had showered and had breakfast sent up to his suite. Shortly after he had finished eating at just after nine o'clock, his phone buzzed in his pocket. He put down his coffee cup to answer it.

"Everything is as it should be, Herr Woolacott," Grindt said into the phone. "We are ready for your inspection."

"Very good," came the reply. "I shall be there within the hour." Switching off his mobile phone, Woolacott picked up his overnight case and left his plush hotel room, an executive suite which had a panoramic view across the Old Botanical Garden and the rooftops of the city. He walked briskly along the thick, carpeted corridor with a contented smile etched across his gnarled face. His chauffeur, having been summoned, was waiting outside the main doors and nodded in greeting as he opened the rear door of the Mercedes that had been provided for his use during his stay. Fifteen minutes later they entered the vehicle testing complex through the guarded gates and came to a halt beside the huge workshop that he had left the day before. This time, there were two armed men at the door of the warehouse building. Woolacott went inside and stopped. Martin Grindt moved toward him with a satisfied smile.

"I have personally inspected the vehicle, Herr Woolacott," Grindt told him. "You will find no outward difference in any conceivable way. The only change is that the steering mechanism, chassis and front wheel on the vehicle now shows no sign of any explosive device nor any trace of explosive material." Lord Woolacott strolled calmly around the vehicle for nearly ten minutes before finally stopping in front of it and nodding his satisfaction.

"Thank you, Herr Grindt," Woolacott said with a smile. "Her Majesty's Government will be most pleased at your work and with the report that you will no doubt file in due course. Arrangements have been made for the agreed remuneration to be made at the earliest convenience but, as I'm sure you are aware, of necessity the wheels turn exceedingly slowly in these matters."

"Of course, Your Lordship, I understand perfectly. These things take time." Martin Grindt had no idea that only three days after making the report that Woolacott had ordered that he would 'fall' from a high gantry at the same testing centre and be killed instantly, nor that the two unsuspecting men who had assisted him throughout that night would be killed in an horrific 'accident' on the fast moving autobahn on their way home from the centre. Lord Andrew Woolacott was highly efficient in arranging his work and having others carry out his instructions.

He arrived in Paris late that afternoon and was taken by chauffeur driven car straight to the Hotel George V, one of the best in the city. That evening, he was joined for dinner in the privacy of his room by Marcel Deschamps, the most senior government pathologist in the country.

"I assume you have been brought up to date, Monsieur Deschamps?" Woolacott asked, his bushy eyebrows raised as they sampled the finest Chablis that preceded their meal.

"Please, call me Marcel," the man responded with a warm smile. "I am, as you say, up to date with developments, Your Lordship."

"If we are dropping formalities, call me Andrew," he said, pouring more wine. "Our best option, and the one that my own superiors favour, would be for the driver, Henri Paul, to be shown to have consumed a large amount of alcohol prior to driving the vehicle in question." The Frenchman appeared to think about the proposition for a moment before giving his answer.

"I do not see why there should be any problem with coming to that conclusion in my report," he said then continued. "And the lady?" Woolacott twisted his glass by its stem as it sat on the table between them. He did not look up as he replied.

26

"It is hoped that in the autopsy there will be no trace of any adverse medication and that death would only have occurred as a direct result of any injuries that she may have sustained in the collision."

"Of course, Andrew. I understand completely. You can be assured that my very thorough report will show exactly that. I have received my orders from the very highest authority, as you can no doubt imagine." Woolacott nodded his approval and understanding of the situation.

"I must say, this is an excellent wine," he said with a smile, holding the glass up to the light to inspect the clarity.

Having been assured that everything was proceeding as required, Woolacott returned to London the next day, his spirits up-lifted from his foreign journey. Upon landing at London City Airport, he was whisked through Customs and Immigration without delay by security officers and into his Daimler limousine. His first stop was Number Ten Downing Street where he was expected by the Prime Minister. Over a splendid lunch, he brought the premier up to date with the operation. The man was exceptionally pleased at how well everything had gone but a little perplexed that James Hogg had not, as yet, been apprehended or eliminated.

* * * *

TOTTENHAM, LONDON

26TH SEPTEMBER 1997

Over the following two weeks, Hogg had given careful consideration to Randall's suggestion. The more he thought about it, the better it sounded. By now there were a lot of conspiracy theories coming up about the so-called accident. Even some of the daily papers were mentioning it. He decided to go for it. The idea of retiring abroad, Spain perhaps, with a fair bit of wedge was a good incentive. Buying a copy of a well known tabloid newspaper, he carefully leafed through it and found the name of one of their investigative journalists. Hogg dialled the number of the paper from the phone box on the corner of Lordship Lane.

"I need to speak to Gary Briers," he told the female who answered his call.

"I'll put you through to his desk, sir, although I'm not sure if he's in his office at the moment," she politely told him. "Please hold the line." The internal phone was answered before the second ring.

"Briers," said a bored voice, stifling a yawn.

"Is that Gary Briers?" Hogg asked unnecessarily. He was still rather nervous about telling his story, especially to someone he didn't know.

"Yes, it is."

"My name is.... er.... Smith," said Hogg, "and I've got the scoop of the century for you if the price is right."

"Really?" Briers responded, raising his weary eyes to the ceiling. "That's the fifth one this week and it's only Tuesday."

"Yeah, well this one is for real," Hogg persisted, beginning to feel somewhat frustrated. "It concerns the Government, the security services and .... er .... a very well known and important family." Briers let his feet fall from his desk and sat up, leaning forward and dropping his voice very slightly. There was something in this man's

28

voice that intrigued him and besides, his reporter's nose was twitching. He was smelling a story in the unfolding.

"Tell me a little more about this scoop, Mister Smith." He knew this was not the man's real name but was happy to play along for the time being.

"There's no way I can tell you anything over the phone," the man said, "and when you hear what I've got to say, you'll understand why."

"So what do you propose then?" Briers asked. Hogg remained silent for a moment, trying to think up the best plan for himself.

"There's a small pub in Tottenham, in a place called Scotland Green," he said at length. "It's called The Two Brewers. I'll be in there at one o'clock tomorrow afternoon and I'll be carrying a copy of The Times. I can guarantee I'll be the only one with a copy of The Times in *there*."

"Alright, Mister Smith," said Briers, having nothing much else to occupy him. He was a little miffed that most of his colleagues were covering stories about Diana's death. "I'll meet you there tomorrow at one."

"Make sure you come alone and if you're not there by quarter past, I'll be gone and so will this story," Hogg told him and quickly hung up the receiver. He was shaking as he left the booth and walked briskly back to his flat.

The following afternoon found Hogg seated in his maroon Sierra outside a minicab office in Scotland Green shortly before twelve thirty. From this point he could watch the door of the pub without being seen. His car blended in with the other minicabs parked there. At five to one, a black cab pulled into the road and stopped outside the pub. A man got out and paid the driver. Hogg guessed him to be in his late thirties, about five feet ten tall and quite stocky with ginger hair and glasses. He went inside as the cab made a U-turn and drove away. Hogg got out of his car and waited a further five minutes to check that no-one else unfamiliar had entered the cul-de-sac. Satisfied, he entered the bar and saw Briers seated at a small round table at the far end, beneath the dart board. He sat down opposite the man and dropped his copy of The Times on the table, nervously looking over his shoulder.

"I'm assuming that you're Gary Briers?" he enquired.

"And you must be Mister Smith," Briers responded with a smile. The landlord, Malcolm, sniggered from behind the bar, for he had known Jimmy Hogg for many years. Hogg shot the balding man a withering look that told him to mind his own business and keep quiet. He turned back to Briers who, in his tan coloured suit looked decidedly out of place in the dingy, back street public house.

"We can't talk here," Hogg told him. "My car's outside." He got up and walked towards the door to the street, checking that the reporter was following him. Briers drained the last of his half pint of lager and followed, getting into Hogg's car as he started the engine.

"Before we go anywhere, Mister Smith, I'd like to know something about this so called scoop of yours."

"Well, Smith's not my real name for a start."

"I *had* managed to work that out."

Hogg swung the car out into the main road then turned right at the lights and drove to the end of Lansdowne Road before pulling into some lock-up garages. He killed the engine and turned to face his passenger. He felt sure they would not be disturbed there, as well as being away from prying eyes.

"You're gonna think this is completely mad when I tell you," he began, "but I gotta tell you, I'm looking for a nice few quid for this story."

"I can't talk about money until I know what's involved, so let's hear it." Hogg appeared slightly uncomfortable as he shifted in his seat and checked behind them, took a deep breath and began his tale.

"Well, …. this is how it all started, …..." It took him over half an hour to relate his story to the reporter, who remained silent and just listened. He missed out nothing and repeated almost verbatim every word that had been said in Lord Woolacott's study. When he had finished, Briers lit a cigarette and simply stared straight ahead through the windscreen at the flaking, pale blue garage doors in front of them. It sounded too fantastic and yet there was something about Hogg, his sincerity, that was all too believable. There had been several rumours whispered around various journalistic circles, but nothing of any substance .... until now.

"If what you've just told me *is* true," said Briers, thoughtfully with a frown, blowing out a stream of smoke through the open window, "then this really *could* be the scoop of the century." He

30

threw the butt of his burned down cigarette out and scribbled away frantically in his notebook for a full five minutes.

"So when do I get my money?" Hogg asked eagerly.

"I'll have to run all this past my boss, the editor," came the reply amidst more scribbling. "He's the one who has to approve any payment, providing there is truth in it all," he concluded, glancing sideways at the informant.

"It's all true," said Hogg, "on my mother's life it is." Briers felt inclined to believe the man.

"Well for a start, we've got to be able to trust each other. Give me your real name and tell me how I can get in touch with you." Hogg hesitated for a moment then asked the question that had been playing on his mind.

"Is it really necessary to have my real name?"

"It is if you want my paper's money." That was enough. Hogg gave the man his real name and his phone number back at his flat. He dropped Briers off back in Scotland Green and watched as he left in a minicab from Miniways cab office. The reporter had promised to call Hogg the next morning with his editor's decision.

When he arrived at his office building, Briers almost ran to the lift. He went straight past his own floor and up to the editor's office. The editor at that time was Sir Richard Slipper, known to all behind his back as Slippery Dick.

"Can he see me immediately please? It's very urgent," Briers told Wendy, the middle aged spinster who sat behind the desk in the outer office. As his secretary of many years and personal assistant, she was Slipper's first line of defence and screened all potential visitors. Briers thought that she should have been seated behind sandbags with a machine gun in front of her.

"What do you want him for, Gary? He's very busy, you know", she asked, hardly looking up from her paperwork.

"I think I may have the biggest story this paper has ever run with," he replied with a huge grin. She picked up a green telephone and pressed a button.

"Gary Briers to see you, Sir Richard. He says it's very urgent." After listening for a couple of seconds, she replaced the receiver and nodded in the direction of the heavy, panelled door. "He says you can have three minutes," she told him with only the merest hint of a smile that barely moved her thin lips. Briers knocked then went straight in.

"What is this all about, Gary?" Slipper demanded, tapping the end of a pen impatiently on his expansive, paper-strewn desk. Briers proceeded to relate the story that Hogg had told him, referring once or twice to his notes. The three minutes came and went without either of them noticing. Slipper's thick cigar, resting in the groove of an ashtray had long since gone out by the time Briers had come to the end.

"And this Hogg fellow is looking for some kind of payment for this story, I take it?" Slipper asked when Briers had finished.

"He says he thinks it's worth a six figure sum," Briers replied with a slow nod of his head. "I don't know about that much money, but I feel we should make him a reasonable offer for his trouble. After all, he could have easily gone to one of the other tabloids with the story."

"Very true," Sir Richard conceded with a slight frown, "we'll see. Leave this with me for the time being, Gary. Keep all this to yourself just for the moment. Not a word to anyone, my lad, and I do mean *anyone*. It's too hot to be bandied around." He sat back in his swivel chair and nodded in the direction of the door, indicating that Briers should now leave the office. Slipper leaned his shirt-sleeved elbows on his leather topped desk and allowed his fingers to meet, almost prayer-like, thinking. After two or three minutes of contemplation he picked up his green telephone and spoke to his secretary in the outer office.

"Wendy, get Lord Woolacott at M.I.5. on the line, would you?" He leaned back once more and waited. Less than a minute later the phone rang and he picked it up, choosing his words very carefully. "Andrew," he said in the friendliest of manner. "Richard Slipper here. Any chance we can meet up somewhere? It is rather important and somewhat hush-hush."

"Up to my eyes in it at the moment, old boy," came the response. "As you can imagine, all hell has broken loose with this Paris thing, you know?"

"Yes, I can imagine," Slipper replied.

"Besides which," Woolacott continued, "I can't tell you anything more about it than you already know."

"Of course, of course." Slipper took a hesitant pause before continuing. "The thing is, I've got hold of a story that sort of, well, …. implicates your department and I feel I should run it by you before I take any action. It *does* actually have a tentative connection to the Paris event." He knew he had the peer's attention now. "Shall we say dinner at my club in Pall Mall at seven thirty?"

"A free dinner would do no harm, I suppose, might even be interesting, depending on what you have. I shall be there." Lord Andrew Woolacott slowly replaced the receiver and sat back in his chair. What did Slipper have up his sleeve? He was certain that no-one from his department had been the cause of any leaks. Steps had been taken to ensure that. Yet Slipper, he knew, was a wily old bark and he wouldn't have called unless he had something of importance. He picked up the internal phone, depressed a button and waited for his P.A. to answer.

"Connie," he said when she answered, "will you ask Zulu if he would come up here immediately, please?" 'Zulu' was the operational name for Roger Whitehead, his second-in-command who had masterminded and overseen the entire covert operation in Paris from conception to horrific end. Some five minutes later he entered Woolacott's plush, sound-proofed office and seated himself in front of the desk. He was dressed in his trademark dark grey, pin-striped suit, pale blue shirt and yellow tie. A flash of gold sparkled from his cuff-links which matched his tie-tack. He flicked his fashionably long, sandy hair back and smiled at his superior.

Whitehead was only just thirty nine years old, willowy, six feet three tall and had been with section five of Military Intelligence for sixteen years, slowly yet methodically working his way up through the junior ranks to his present elevated position. From his humble beginnings as a lowly, twenty three year old filing clerk he had come far and learned from the very best in the business. He had his eyes firmly set on the coveted position that Lord Woolacott currently held.

"You wanted to see me, Andrew?"

"Indeed I did, Roger," he said, thoughtfully. "Any small chance that there could have been some kind of leakage from anyone, do you think? Any remote possibility that someone from the Department could have let something slip to anyone at all? Anything that any one of the newspapers could have got hold of? They only need the merest hint to get them started."

"Absolutely impossible. Everything was done on a need to know basis and those few that *were* in the know have been adequately taken care of, one way or another. Even the photographer and driver of the motorcycle who detonated the device is out of the picture, so to speak. Had a very nasty, …. er, …. accident on the Yamaha on the A.16 autoroute on their way back to Calais. Hit by a rather large articulated truck travelling at great speed, apparently. Killed outright. I very much doubt if anything was leaked from the German end either. Martin Grindt at Mercedes had too much to lose, as you know. Our contacts in Paris are secure also. Why do you ask?"

Lord Woolacott told him about the recent telephone call from Slipper and asked for his thoughts on the matter.

"Well, there are always going to be conspiracy theories, we expected something like that," Whitehead replied. "You well know what these newspaper men are like, Andrew. He's probably heard something and is simply fishing, hoping to get a scoop or a head start on the other papers."

"You may be right. Let us hope that is all there is to it. I'll have dinner with him and see what comes from it."

* * * *

PALL MALL, LONDON

24TH. SEPTEMBER 1997

That evening, Sir Richard Slipper waited until they were sipping their brandies after the dessert before broaching the subject that had brought them together. Woolacott understood the etiquette of these matters very well. Slipper related what he had been told by Gary Briers and sat back contentedly, watching the intelligence chief through the haze of blue smoke from his rather expensive cigar. He was hoping to see the spy chief squirm but the man remained calm and studied the editor.

"Nothing in it at all, naturally, old chap," Woolacott responded after a mere moment's hesitation. "This chap, er .... Hogg did you say his name was? He's quite obviously simply trying to rip you off for a few pounds." He puffed away on his own cigar for a time, studying Slipper carefully through the billowing smoke. "Of course, this is a story that you can not possibly print, Richard, as I'm sure you realise. It would simply fuel these other outrageous rumours doing the rounds." He stubbed out his cigar and leaned forward. "By the way, Richard," he said with a wry smile, looking directly at the newspaper man's face across the table, "I'm considering having a word with the powers that be about putting your name forward for a peerage in the upcoming Honours List. Would that be something of interest for you? Strictly off the record, at the moment, you understand?" He held the editor's gaze unswervingly. They both knew what was being offered here, although unspoken.

"Yes, Andrew, it most certainly would," Sir Richard replied, nodding. They both left the club some ten minutes later and stood at the top of the steps in Pall Mall. Woolacott's car was waiting at the kerb and Slipper looked hopefully along the road for a vacant cab with it's yellow light on.

"I can see that you are probably right about Hogg," Slipper said, as the uniformed concierge waved his white gloved arm in the air at a distant taxi. "I'll see to it that the story, such as it is, remains buried. I'll put Briers on to something substantial, probably overseas to keep him occupied."

"Quite right, Richard. Oh, ….just as an afterthought, let me have everything you have on this Hogg chappie, just so that I can look him up on our systems. Can't have these scaremongers running around unchecked, can we?"

The black cab pulled in to the kerb behind Woolacott's Daimler and Slipper got in, giving the driver the address of his mistress in Putney. Due to the lateness of the hour, he decided to favour her with his company that night. As the cab pulled away he couldn't but help smiling to himself. A peerage, no less. His wife would wet her knickers at the thought of him getting in to the House of Lords. Lord Slipper? He liked the sound of that. He thought that he may even get his leg across when she heard the news tomorrow. A rare occurrence these days.

As for Lord Woolacott, he used his coded mobile phone to make a call. It rang three times before being answered. He instructed Roger Whitehead to meet him at his offices immediately.

"It's going to take me three quarters of an hour at least I'm afraid, Andrew," he informed His Lordship with reluctance. He didn't like to get on his wrong side. "At the moment I'm just about to get into the shower."

"Leave the shower until later, man. This is *urgent*," came the retort. The line went dead before he had the chance to make a reply. Twenty five minutes later he was entering his superior's office. Woolacott immediately recounted his conversation with the editor over dinner and asked for ideas.

"It appears to me," Whitehead stated, "that a small-time cat burglar like him could very easily disappear without trace, or perhaps fall from the roof of a building he was in the process of breaking in to."

"Jolly good idea, Roger," Woolacott nodded. "I'll leave it all in your capable hands, but do keep me informed, won't you? There are certain people, much higher than me who want this whole thing kept under wraps, as I'm sure you understand. I in turn have to report to them and this latest development will not please them at all."

"I understand completely, Andrew. Leave it with me and I'll put the necessary wheels in motion immediately," Whitehead replied with a warm smile and turned on his heels, quietly leaving the office and closing the door softly behind him. When he reached his own domain on the floor below, he turned his attention to his computer and very soon had before him all the details he needed on James Arthur Hogg. He dialled an internal number as he continued to take in all the information on the screen. When the call was answered, he asked for Paul Gosling to be sent up to him. Five minutes later his door opened without a knock and a well built man in his early thirties entered, walked across the room and leaned casually with his backside against the window sill, one hand unbuttoning his suit jacket, his tie loosened and hanging a little crookedly. He looked down at his superior officer with an air of impudence, a sort of 'couldn't care less' attitude. Almost as if *he* was the most senior man in the room. Standing well over six feet tall with a square shaped, shaven head, he looked every bit as menacing as he was supposed to, given the difficult tasks he was employed for.

"I'm assuming you have a disposal job for me," said Paul Gosling. It was a statement rather than a question. He had been a senior part of Whitehead's disposal team for almost three years and had performed his tasks well. Twenty three people had vanished without trace or met with untimely deaths by accidents under his supervision. Whitehead was always a little afraid of Gosling. There was something ruthless, almost primeval about the him. Man or woman, it made no difference to Gosling. It was just his job and he carried out his work with an enthusiasm that Whitehead found a little unnerving. It was the amount of ruthlessness that his boss was wary of.

"For God's sake, sit down, will you? This is what I want done." He proceeded to give his henchman all the information he had on Hogg, without mentioning the break-in or the overheard conversation between himself and Lord Woolacott. That was information that Gosling had no need to know of. When he had finished, he emphasised the importance of the task he was setting. "I want this one gone as quickly as possible, Gosling," he said. "Every resource within the Department is at your disposal. This one is truly a matter of national security, believe me. It concerns this department's involvement in the Paris thing just recenetly. These top secret orders come from the very highest office you could imagine."

"I'll get on to it first thing in the morning." Gosling already had an idea that Five was implicated in the accident. He always had his ear to the ground and very little passed without his knowledge.

"You'll damned well get on to it right *now*," Whitehead shouted back at the man. He wasn't happy about any of the news getting out as it obviously had.

"Okay, chief," Gosling responded with an audible sigh. "Can I get Special Branch involved too?"

"*No*! *Definitely not*!" Whitehead said, still shouting. "I know they are all P.V.'d but you never know. This is far too sensitive to take the chance. 'Positive Vetting' or not, it only takes one careless word and this entire operation will be at risk. We'll keep it to ourselves for the time being. Oh, and while you're at it, let's have this reporter chappie, Gary Briers, put under twenty four hour surveillance too, it's possible we may find Hogg through him." It was going to be another long night, trawling through computers and all the thousands of records that were available to the Intelligence Services. Whitehead was diligent though. He had to be to have reached his elevated position within the department known internally as Section Five.

The following morning at eleven fifteen, Sir Richard Slipper was addressing Gary Briers, his investigative reporter.

"I've been in touch with people all morning, Gary, and it seems that James Hogg has tried this sort of scam a number of times before. Apparently, one of the red-top tabloids actually paid him fifteen grand for a story that turned out to be completely false" he lied with conviction. "He told them that he had evidence of a Government plot that killed Lord Louis Mountbatten in Ireland many years back. The man seems hell-bent on making money from newspapers with unfounded allegations. The man's a total scoundrel. Anyway," he continued, averting his eyes and needlessly shuffling reams of papers on his desk, "forget about him. You'll be going out to Australia within a day or two. Place called Katoomba in the Blue Mountains, New South Wales. There's been reports of a British girl living rough in the mountains near there. Been living wild there for nearly four years, by all accounts. I'd like you to see what you can make of the story. You're booked in to The Metropole on the corner of Lurline

Street in Katoomba" Gary Briers did not even blink. His nose was twitching again and he was certain there was more to this Hogg affair than Slippery Dick was letting on. He didn't trust his editor one iota and figured that someone on high had got to him since their previous meeting. Instead of disagreeing, he simply nodded his obedience.

"No probs, Guv," he said. "As long as you can give me a day or two to put my affairs in order first."

"Yes, that should be okay. Let me know when you're ready and I'll get the tickets arranged for you. The hotel's booked for next Thursday for seven nights. Should give you enough time to get the story."

Briers took the lift down to the lobby and left the building. He walked a hundred yards or so round the corner, went into a public phone booth and dialled the number Hogg had given him.

"Jimmy? This is Briers," he said when the call was answered. "Meet me at the same place as before in exactly one hour. Take a circuitous route and keep looking in your mirror. Make *sure* you're not followed, understand?"

"Er .... yeah .... okay," Hogg replied, feeling a little concerned now. "Nothing wrong with getting my bit of dough, is there?"

"Just *be* there! And watch your back." Briers hung up without another word, leaving Hogg staring at the handset buzzing in his hand. This was not going as planned as far as Hogg was concerned. He was the kind of man who would cast his bread upon the waters and expect to retrieve it after many days not only buttered but with a thick coating of jam. He wasn't used to all this cloak-and-dagger stuff that Briers had insisted upon. It was getting to be hard work, something that Hogg was not used to. He looked at his fake Rolex watch. Ten past twelve. He pulled on his jacket for there was a slight chill in the air for that time of the year. Locking the door behind him, he went downstairs to his trusty Ford, started up and pulled away. He drove just over the speed limit up to the A.10 and headed north along the dual carriageway. Checking his rear view mirror frequently, he eventually came to Southbury Road and turned left, then left again into the slip road that ran alongside the main road. Turning left once again at the end, he jumped the lights on amber and put his foot to the floor, under the railway bridge then going right and weaving in and out of a maze of side roads. He arrived back at

Scotland Green at exactly one o'clock and parked at the far end, facing out with the engine running.

Briers had got off the train at Bruce Grove some ten minutes earlier and walked the rest of the way. He kept looking over his shoulder and darting in and out of shops and side streets to make certain that no-one was following. It was only five minutes after the allotted time that he arrived at The Two Brewers. Hogg had seen him enter the cul-de-sac and moved his car forward to meet the reporter.

"Get us away from here, Jimmy," he said urgently as he dived into the front passenger seat, "and make it quick." Hogg realised that something was terribly wrong from the tone of Gary's voice and threw the car into gear. He drove to a nearby Sainsburys supermarket, pulled up in the car park and switched off. Neither of them noticed the battered yet souped-up, dark green Mini-van that eased into a parking space half a dozen places along from them, nor did they see the long camera lens that protruded from the passenger window.

"So what the fuck's going on here, Gary?" Hogg asked, his voice faint and quivering with fear. Briers told him what had happened with his editor and of his suspicions that the man had been told by someone on high to smother the story.

"The thing is, Jimmy," Briers told him, "if Slippery Dick has passed on your story to the Intelligence Service, which I now suspect he most certainly has, your life could very well be in danger."

"But why?" Hogg screamed. "All I wanted was a few quid to keep my mouth shut. I'm not going to be yelling it from the rooftops, am I?" The cat burglar was sweating profusely at that point, despite the chill outside the car.

"Maybe nothing will happen at all, or maybe you'll just get a visit from someone to warn you off. On the other hand, they may not want to risk it and want to put you out of the picture for good, just in case."

"Fuck me!" Hogg exclaimed. "This is starting to get a bit too heavy for my liking. Can't I just tell them that I don't want anything to do with it? That I'm not bothered what they get up to?"

"I don't think so, mate. You would always be a constant worry for them. They'll always have the fear of you opening your mouth at some stage in the future, can't you see that? I reckon your best bet is to get abroad for a while, let things die down a bit, maybe even get the story out in another country."

"*Abroad*? You're fucking *joking*, pal. Where will I get *that* sort of money? I haven't got a pot to piss in at the moment." Briers could see the man's point and was deep in thought for a while before speaking.

"Look," he said at length, "if we can get this story out, maybe in a foreign newspaper, they wouldn't dare touch you then. It would be too obvious. I've got a friend who works on one of the French papers. I'll get him to meet us at the Gare Du Nord in Paris." He handed Hogg a piece of paper with a number on it. "Stay away from your flat and ring me on that number at ten tomorrow morning from a different phone. That number I've just given you is a phone box so if it's engaged, keep trying until you get through, okay? It's possible that they've got your home phone tapped." Hogg folded the scrap of paper and slid it into his inside pocket.

"Alright, I'll ring at ten on the dot."

"Good. Now drop me off at the station." They turned right out of the car park and the green Mini van followed, four cars behind. When Briers reached Bruce Grove Station, he went up the steps and sat down on a bench halfway along the platform. He barely gave a glance at the middle aged couple, arm in arm, who came up the steps behind and waited, like him, for the next train to the London terminus. When he arrived at Liverpool Street Station he walked to the taxi rank and it was only as he got in that he noticed the same couple boarding the taxi behind his. As his own cab made off, he kept glancing nonchalantly through the rear window. He felt certain that the same cab was following his own. As he arrived at his offices, getting out to pay the driver he looked along the road and saw the other cab pull into the kerb some two hundred yards away. It did not bode well that no-one disembarked.

Briers stood just inside the foyer of his building and kept watch from behind a pillar and through the tinted glass frontage. After ten minutes, the man and woman alighted from the black cab and got in to a dark blue Vauxhall Omega that had pulled in and stopped behind the stationary taxi. That was enough for Briers. He now knew for certain that he was being watched by professionals. He had done enough surveillance work himself to know.

At precisely that moment, Hogg was sitting on the edge of his bed, biting his nails to the quick and frightened almost to death at the way things were going. He just wanted out of the whole thing now. Why had he listened to that pratt, Randall? He stuffed a couple of shirts, some T-shirts, a pair of trousers, one pair of jeans, some underwear and socks into a holdall. That very nearly accounted for his entire wardrobe. Pulling on his black leather jacket, he slid his passport into the inside pocket along with his Lloyds debit card. He tried to ring his sister in Edmonton but got no answer and so instead, using some of the cash he had secreted beneath one of the floorboards for an emergency, went to a bed and breakfast hotel in Philip Lane to spend the night.

The next morning at exactly ten o'clock, using the pay-phone in the B & B, he dialled the number of the call box that Briers had given him. The man answered immediately.

"I've got to get you away as quickly as possible, Jimmy, and we need to talk in depth without any risk of being overheard or taped," Briers told him in an urgent manner. "Things are happening which we need to discuss. Do you know the Jack Straw's Castle pub in Hampstead?"

"Yeah, I've seen it. It's near the pond," Hogg replied.

"That's right. Now halfway down the hill going towards Golders Green is another pub called the Bull and Bush. Do you know that one?" Hogg knitted his brows and tried to think.

"I think I know the place," he eventually said.

"Right, now listen very carefully to what I'm about to tell you," Briers said, almost in a whisper. "Behind that pub, on some waste land, you will see a small, grey, concrete block-house, no windows, just a metal door set into one side. I'm sure someone with your expertise will have no problem with the lock. Inside, you will find a spiral staircase which goes down to the old, disused Bull and Bush underground station. You'll need a torch. I'll meet you down there on the platform some time between two and six. I can't be more specific as I have to be extra careful myself. I've been tailed since I left you in Tottenham and possibly before that."

"Christ on a bike!" Hogg exclaimed in disbelief. "I don't like the fucking sound of this, Gary."

"Just make sure you're there." Briers hung up and looked around before leaving the booth. There was no way he could have known that he had been seen using that same phone box the previous day and that the line was now constantly monitored. A man at MI5 headquarters adjusted his head-phones back around his neck and picked up the telephone by his elbow.

Within minutes of Briers making his phone call, Whitehead knew everything he had said in the conversation. He summoned Gosling to his office immediately with further precise instructions. Gosling knew exactly what had to be done and left to get on with the business of selecting the right team to assist him. There were now going to be three persons that urgently required his professional attention; Hogg, Briers and now Sir Richard Slipper. Someone was going to be having an 'accident'. Too many people were in the know and that number had to be drastically reduced at the earliest opportunity.

* * * *

HAMPSTEAD, LONDON

24TH. SEPTEMBER 1997

At the Tottenham branch of Lloyds Bank, Hogg withdrew all of his money held there, a little over three thousand pounds. Then, taking a circuitous route, he drove to Golders Green at a leisurely pace and parked in a side street several hundred yards from the station. He had taken great care to ensure that he had not been followed, doubling back on himself, checking his mirrors constantly and even jumping red lights on two occasions. Walking through a number of residential roads with his hold-all slung over one shoulder, he came out almost opposite Golders Green tube station. He turned right on to North End Road and, walking briskly, after ten minutes arrived at the Bull and Bush public house. To one side of the pub was a patch of waste ground, overgrown with weeds and brambles and surrounded by spiked iron railings. He threw his bag over and hauled himself up between the spikes, dropping down on the other side. Traffic sped past in both directions but, as far as he could ascertain, no-one appeared to be taking any interest in his activities. Moving swiftly into the cover of the long grass, he collected his bag and began to make his way towards a small building, covered in ivy, that he had spotted from the roadway. As Briers had said, a rusting, heavy metal door was set into it on the far side, out of sight of the main road. A huge, industrial padlock secured the outward opening door. One look was enough to tell Hobbs that it would be a difficult but not impossible task to open it. Laying his bag beside him, he bent to the lock with his set of pickers. It took him a little over three minutes to get the lock released and all his strength to pull the door far enough open to squeeze inside, due to the mass of weeds and grass that had accumulated against it. Tugging it closed again behind him was no less difficult.

It was pitch black inside, a stale odour pervading the atmosphere.

He switched on his pencil torch and located the spiral metal staircase that stretched steeply down ahead of him. The luminous dial on his watch showed a quarter past one. As he went carefully down the steps, he heard the sound of a train rumbling far beneath him and stopped for a moment. After the noise of the train abated, he could hear water dripping somewhere further down, a steady, rhythmic plopping sound. It took him a good fifteen minutes at a slow, cautious pace to reach the bottom and the beam from his torch reached out into the darkness before him. He was on the platform, littered with scraps of paper and debris, thick with dust. He could even make out some of the old advertisements on the walls. Park Drive cigarettes? When had he last seen *them in the shops*? Years ago. He heard another train approaching and was buffeted by the blast of warm air being pushed along in front of its blunt cab through the tunnel. Switching off his torch, he ducked down as the front of the train entered the station. He need not have bothered. No-one would have seen him in the dark even if they had been looking out of the windows. Nobody ever did on the tube for there was nothing to see. The lights in the carriages flashed past him and he could clearly see the passengers in their seats, some reading, others chatting, all of them oblivious to his presence. Dust swirled up in little tornadoes all along the platform as he turned his torch on again and he noticed some of the scraps of paper were being sucked into the tunnel behind the train. Hogg stood up, brushing dust and dirt from his jeans. He found a passageway leading off the platform at the far end. He went inside the entrance and sat down on the ground, leaning his back against the wall to wait. Everything seemed to be covered in a film of dust.

Over the next two and a half hours that he sat there, he was disturbed only by the trains that were so frequent that he no longer even glanced at them. There was also the occasional large, brown rat that scurried past him. He shone his light at them but after a brief glance in his direction, their yellowing eyes illuminated in the beam, they ignored him and went about their business. He had just looked at his watch for perhaps the twentieth time, five to four, when he heard footsteps coming down the staircase he himself had used some time earlier. The beam of a torch flooded the platform at the far end then swung along the wall towards him. Hogg stood up, remaining hidden just inside the passageway and listened. A half whispered voice reached him, echoing back and forth from the arched walls.

"Hogg? ..... You there? ..... Jimmy, it's me, ... Gary." Hogg switched on his own torch and shone it straight into the other man's eyes, temporarily blinding him. He put a hand up to shield his eyes. "Is that you, Hogg?"

"Course it is, unless you were expecting someone else." Briers walked towards him.

"We've got to get you out of the country as soon as possible, today," he said as he approached.

"I'm worried about all this, Gary," Hobbs whined in reply.

"Either that or you'll end up on a slab. There are powerful forces behind all this as you've probably guessed," Briers told him. "I've been continuously watched and I'm pretty sure my office phone is being tapped. It's only a matter of time before they find you."

"What am I going to do? If you're right, they'll have all the ports and airports on alert as well."

"I know, don't worry. I've got a good friend called George, he's got a fishing boat called the Joanne-Marie at Folkestone in Kent. He's agreed to get you over to France, then you can get the train into Paris. You'll be met there by one of my French colleagues, Henri. This is his phone number." Briers handed across a slip of paper torn from his notebook. He's *very* interested in what you've told me. He will keep you somewhere safe until the story comes out into the open."

"Alright, I suppose," Hogg said with more than a little trepidation. "Can we trust him, do you think?"

"I'd stake my life on it, he's a good man. Have you got money?" Briers enquired.

"Yeah, I've got just under five grand in cash plus my debit card. There's another two thousand there."

"Don't use that card," Briers ordered him. "They can trace any withdrawals as soon as you use it. Now, this is the plan, ..."

Before he could continue, there was a sudden rush of warm, stale air from the tunnel again, accompanied by the sound of another train approaching. This time though, the noise was not as loud, the train sounded as if it was going slower than any of the previous ones. The blunt cab of the train entered the station as they watched, slowing almost to a halt. As it did so, in the pale, reflected glow of the carriage lights, Hogg saw the driver's door open and three men leaped onto the platform. No sooner had they exited the cab than the train accelerated sharply and in seconds was vanishing through the opposite tunnel. A powerful spotlight swiftly scanned the unlit platform areas and Hogg threw himself sideways into the passageway beside him. He rolled over once and regained his balance in a kneeling position just as the spotlight fell upon Briers, illuminating him like a rabbit caught in a car's headlights. At almost the same instant, two shots rang out in quick succession. A small hole opened in the centre of the reporter's forehead and another just slightly above his right eye, shattering his spectacles and sending them flying. The force also threw him backwards and he fell in a crumpled heap at Hogg's feet, his ginger hair listing across his forehead covered in his own sticky blood. The noise of the silenced gun reverberated around the empty station.

Hogg felt his bowels loosening as he frantically scrambled to his feet in a panic and ran headlong down the passageway he was in, not knowing where it would lead him or indeed, if it led anywhere at all. Maybe all the exits were now blocked up. Risking a quick look back over his shoulder as he stumbled along, his hand felt the often damp, tiled walls to guide him. Seeing the beam of their powerful torch playing across the entrance of the passage behind him spurred him on as well as the sound of their running feet. Suddenly, he hit a brick wall in front of him and, seeing a faint glow to his right, turned in that direction. As he stumbled on, he found as he neared the source of the glow that he was in another, wider passage. Without warning, he came out on to a different platform with several inspection lights strung out at hundred yard intervals along the far side of the tracks. So sudden was it that he only just managed to stop himself from falling over the edge of the platform and on to the tracks. He knew from the noises behind that his pursuers were gaining on him and took an instant gamble. Running to the far end of the platform, he dropped down on to the tracks and made his way into the dark tunnel. Thankfully, he found that the string of lights went on for some distance and hoped he could make it into the darkness before the three men got to the platform. Then there was the fear of electrocution from the live rail to contend with as well.

Hogg was sweating profusely when the sound of a train coming from behind filled him with dread. It was then that he noticed a tiny alcove just ahead of him and he squeezed himself in to it with seconds to spare. As he huddled there, the train sped past less than a foot from his face. On the plus side, he thought, there could be no-one behind him on the tracks. Taking his small torch from his pocket, he pointed it in the direction the train had gone. Listening intently for a moment, he was certain there was no pursuit along the tracks and set off at a trot, the torch lighting his way and illuminating the live rail that he feared so much. Within minutes, he could see the lights of another station not too far ahead and he quickened his pace. A couple of tunnels branched off to his right but he ignored them and continued on the main track towards the station before him.

He had no idea what direction he had taken as he had totally lost his bearings in the passages so was not too surprised when he scrambled up on to the platform to find he was at Hampstead. There was, however, a great deal of surprise on the faces of the waiting commuters when a scruffy, dirty man literally rolled over the edge from the rails clutching a bag. Hogg simply grinned at them, pushed his way through and hurried via the connecting passage to the other platform just as a train was pulling in and came to a squeaking halt beside him. As soon as the doors opened, he barged his way on and wedged himself between the standing passengers. After what seemed an age, the doors slid shut and the train pulled away. Hogg reflected on his narrow escape as he travelled through the tunnel. The powers that be had obviously known about the meeting, probably from intercepting their telephone calls and decided to trap him and Briers down there on the station platform. Maybe they were both destined to be killed underground where there were no witnesses. They probably had others waiting at the top of the spiral staircase should either of them manage to escape that way. The three men who had chased him would have been in contact with those on the surface and sent them to Hampstead to cut off his escape there. This was definitely his best bet, he thought. They would never think that he had doubled back the way he had come. Hogg squinted through the grime on the windows, trying to catch a glimpse of the disused station as they passed but to no avail. The train stopped briefly at Golders Green and then continued it's rumbling, swaying

48

journey with Hogg still aboard. There was no way he would go back to his car in case he had been followed or they had located it. A few minutes later, the train pulled in at Brent Cross Station and he pushed his way off the crowded carriage. He ran up to the ticket collector and thrust a ten pound note into the astonished man's hand.

"Ticket machine wouldn't take this, mate," he said and went past the man at a run. He emerged on to Highfield Avenue, not knowing which way to go. An elderly Asian woman came out of the station behind him.

"Where can I get a cab, love?" he asked her.

"End of the road and turn right," she replied, pointing. Following her directions, Hogg came to a minicab office and entered. He was told there would be a twenty minute wait so he settled down on one of the benches against the wall of the small waiting area of the office. It was half an hour later that a cab became available for him. He took the cab to Turin Street in Bethnal Green, East London. Alighting on the corner of the road, he stood there for a while, looking around for anyone suspicious, figures seated in parked cars. Seeing no-one, he set off along the dark street with caution. There were cars parked up along both sides of the street and he carefully studied each one that he passed, looking for shadowy figures lurking within. He saw none and continued to the house he was searching for, still apprehensive.

Roger Whitehead had by now drawn up a comprehensive list of every single one of Hogg's known associates and friends. The task had taken one of his competent researchers some hours and the results sat before him. He called down to one of his subordinates and had him send observers to all the addresses on the list, which severely stretched his manpower. He began to think that he may have to get Woolacott's permission to call in Special Branch for some help using their expertise.

It was fortunate for Whitehead that two of his operatives were keeping watch in Bethnal Green when Hogg arrived. Gerry Lockhead, one of Hogg's old acquaintances lived there with his girlfriend. With a little bit of good fortune and some cash, there might be a car there for him to utilise. He walked swiftly to the door and, with a quick look around, rang the bell.

"Jesus Christ, …. Jimmy!" Gerry exclaimed with genuine

pleasure. "I ain't seen you fer yonks."

"Been a bit busy, mate," Hogg responded with a grin and a knowing wink. "You going to ask me in, or what?"

Lockhead was tall and somewhat gangly with sandy coloured, thinning hair that he wore in a fashionable pony-tail. He had a long face that wore a constant doleful expression. He led Hogg through to a rear living room, sparsely furnished but with a huge television in one corner.

"Thing is, Gerry," Hogg began after declining the offer of a cup of tea, "I'm in a bit of a fix at the moment. Any chance of borrowing a motor for a couple of days? I can bung you a few quid for it."

"Fuck me, Jim," Gerry responded, shaking his head so that his pony-tail swung from side to side, "I don't see you for nearly a year then you turn up out of the blue askin' fer a jam jar."

"Yeah, …. sorry, mate, but I wouldn't be asking if I wasn't so desperate." Hogg pulled a hundred pounds from his side pocket and held it out. "There's a oner there. I've got to get out of London as quick as possible and my car's out of the question."

"Old Bill's lookin' fer yer, I s'pose?" Taking the banknotes and stuffing them into his shirt pocket, Gerry went to the television set and took some keys from the shelf beneath it. Twisting one key from the ring, he handed it to Hogg. "The only one I can let you 'ave, mate," Gerry sighed, "is an old, blue Austin Maxi. It's parked at the end of the street but it'll need some juice, though."

"Cheers, Gerry. I'll let you know where you can pick it up from when I'm finished with it." They sat around for a further twenty minutes, chatting about old times and past scams. Hogg felt he couldn't just turn up, borrow a car and simply leave immediately. Eventually he stood up to leave.

"I've got to go, mate. Places to go, you know?"

"Alright, Jim," Gerry replied. "You take care an' watch yer back. Don't forget to bell me when you've finished with the car. It cost me money, you know, a lot more than a hundred quid." Hogg promised that he would and walked off along the road, the front door slamming noisily behind him. He saw the Austin at the corner on the opposite side of the road and started to cross. As he stepped off the kerb, the doors of a car a hundred yards along were thrown open and two men emerged rapidly. They both wore dark suits and Hogg immediately noticed that one was holding a hand-gun alongside his right leg. They started to move swiftly towards him so he turned and fled in the opposite direction, away from the car he was supposed to be borrowing as fast as his legs would carry him, the fear rising as bile in his throat. Just before he reached the main road, he saw an alleyway on his right and, as he skidded into it, stole a glance over his shoulder. The leading man chasing him was raising the gun.

* * * *

An hour before Hogg had arrived in Bethnal Green, just before dusk, Sir Richard Slipper was driving out of London on the M40 motorway on his way home. He wasn't really thinking about anything in particular, just driving automatically, reflecting on that day's newspaper stories and tomorrow's likely headline banner. As he passed a certain road-sign, he knew from habit that it would only take another fifteen minutes to reach his spacious country house in Buckinghamshire by leaving the motorway at the next exit. A large, flat-bed truck with a trailer carrying a huge crane was travelling in the left hand lane at around sixty miles an hour and so, going only slightly faster than the lorry as was his normal habit, Slipper checked his mirror, indicated and pulled out in to the centre lane. Exactly as expected. The lorry driver saw it in his side mirror and prepared himself. Just as Slipper was about to draw level with the back of the truck, a large Mercedes van came up fast on his off-side and swerved hard to the left, crashing into his right front wing, sending his car careering to his left. At the same time, the driver of the heavy lorry slammed on his air-brakes and Slipper's Lexus saloon smashed into the back of it, almost slicing the roof and windows from his car as the bonnet slid underneath the rear. The light grey van that had deliberately caused the carnage sped away and was lost in the confusion of squealing brakes from other vehicles as every other driver on that road tried to avoid the devastating collision ahead of them and immediately in their path. At the same time, a long nosed tipper lorry, loaded high with gravel that had been deliberately tailing Slipper for the past three miles ploughed into the back of Sir Richard's car at over sixty miles an hour, reducing the Lexus to little more than a cube of mangled metal. Vehicles were strewn all over the busy carriageway as they hit their brakes, skidding, bringing the commuter laden motorway to a complete standstill. There was very

51

little left of the Lexus when the emergency services eventually arrived, having been seriously hampered by the tail-back of traffic. On close inspection of the crushed car, Sir Richard Slipper was found to have been decapitated. The driver of the flat-bed truck claimed that when he saw the accident in his side mirror, he had braked hard in a bid to avoid another collision. The police had no reason to doubt his story and no further action was taken on his part. Likewise, the tipper lorry driver claimed that everything happened so suddenly that he had no time to take evasive action and the resulting smash had been unavoidable.

Enquiries into the grey van drew no results. It had been caught on overhead cameras entering the motorway just behind Slipper's car at the the beginning of the motorway and a subsequent check revealed that it was carrying false number plates and could not be traced. It was never found.

* * * *

EDMONTON, LONDON

25TH SEPTEMBER 1997

Hogg was on the verge of drifting off to sleep on his sister's sofa in Edmonton at a quarter to five when he heard the sound of a slow moving car which caused him to leap painfully to his feet. Peeking through a gap in the curtains, he saw a dark coloured Ford Granada cruising slowly up the road. As he watched, he saw to his horror four faces, all staring at the house as it went by. The car came to a stop behind an old blue Transit van. In the half light of a grey dawn, he saw someone get out of the back of the van and bend to the driver's window of the Granada. Within seconds, Hogg was frantically tugging at the bolt on the back door of the house. He went through and down the garden path like an express train, despite being hampered by his damaged ankle and hurled himself head-first over the wooden slatted fence at the bottom, landing in a flower bed in the garden behind. At a run, he continued down an alleyway between the houses and came out into the adjacent road. Without hesitation, he crossed the road and into another alley, through another back garden and vaulted yet another fence. His ankle was hurting like hell now but he did not dare stop for a breather. His life depended on keeping going. He now found himself in a graveyard behind a huge church. Fitting, he thought, if they caught him there. He weaved in and out of the gravestones, making his way to the main road on the other side of the church. A main road was nowhere to be if they came looking for him as he knew they would. They wanted him too badly to let him get away now. Limping across and into Winchester Road, he found a man in a turban raising the shutters on a newsagent's shop while another was throwing bundles of newspapers on to the ground from the back of a van. As Hogg approached, the driver got back into his cab. Hogg jumped into the passenger seat beside the startled man just as the engine fired and caught.

"Listen, mate," he told the young man, pulling a twenty pound note from the wad in his pocket. "There's an angry husband chasing after me. Just drop me at your next delivery and this is for your trouble."

The man snatched the offered note and, with a knowing grin crunched the van into gear, burning rubber as he pulled away. Less than a quarter of a mile along the road he stopped outside another shop.

"This is my last drop," the driver told him. "If you want to hang on, I'll drop you off in Enfield Town. That's three miles away so you should be okay from there."

"Lovely, thanks, pal," Hogg replied and sat back with a sigh. A quarter of an hour later found Hogg standing by the roadside in Enfield. All he had in the world was the thick wad of cash in his pocket, his holdall left back at his sister's house in his haste to escape. No passport, no change of clothes, simply what he stood up in. A car approached and he stuck his thumb out hopefully. To his astonishment, the car stopped beside him and the driver leaned over.

"Where do you want to get to, old son?" he asked.

"To the motorway, mate. The M.1." Hogg had the beginning of an idea forming in the back of his mind.

"I can drop you at South Mimms service station if that's any help to you?" Hogg got in and arrived at the service station some twenty minutes later. Treating himself to a burger and a coffee, he wandered out into the truck parking area. He eventually found a driver sitting in his cab, smoking.

"Not going anywhere near Newcastle, are you, mate?" he asked, trying his best to look forlorn.

"Middlesborough," he replied with a broad Midlands accent and gazing down at the bedraggled figure beside his door.

"Any chance of a lift?"

"I'm not supposed to take hitch-hikers."

"Will this change your mind?" Hobbs asked, offering two twenty pound notes.

"Climb up then, me old mate," the overweight driver said, relieving Hogg of the banknotes rather quickly. The big diesel engine roared into life and, turning slowly because of the forty five foot trailer, the lorry made it's way out of the park and edged on to the motorway. By the time the driver had got his truck in to sixth gear, the steady throb of the powerful engine was lulling Hogg into a well needed sleep.

At the same moment that Hogg had scrambled through the churchyard, five well-built men had softly approached Tracy's front door. Two of them peeled off and went down the side of the house to cover the back door. The senior of the other three began pounding on the door with a great deal of force. Before Tracy could get to the top of the stairs, the front door crashed in, almost taking it from it's hinges. She screamed as one of them ran up the stairs towards her.

"Police!" he told her, waving an I.D. card in her horrified, frightened face. It was a lie, of course. "Where is he, love?" the man continued, glaring at her then pushing past.

"Jimmy?" she managed to stammer. "He's downstairs on the sofa."

"Downstairs is clear," came a voice from below, "but the back door was swinging wide open when we got here." Tracy was escorted down the staircase and made to sit at the kitchen table. The two children upstairs were crying now, scared out of their wits.

"Now then, Tracy," said the man who was obviously in charge of the group. "Where would he have gone? You may as well tell me. It would be better for him in the long run, you know."

"I ain't got a clue, honest I ain't. What's he done now anyway?"

"All I can tell you is that he's committed a very serious offence. So serious, in fact, that within the hour every copper in the country will be looking for him." This was not an untruth. Zulu had declared that Hogg should be picked up at the earliest opportunity and had set this task to Special Branch who, in turn, had drawn in every police force in Britain. As far as the police were concerned, Hogg was wanted for espionage as well as the murder of Gary Briers, a well respected Fleet Street reporter in a disused Underground station. This was the story that Whitehead had put behind the arrest warrant. After another hour of questioning, they were satisfied that Tracy had no knowledge of Hogg's whereabouts and withdrew, leaving her sobbing in the chair at her kitchen table, hugging the weeping children.

Paul Gosling sat in the front passenger seat of the Granada and lifted his coded mobile phone. He wasn't relishing making this call.

He knew what happened to people who let Whitehead down too often. His call was answered immediately.

"Zulu," said the voice he knew so well.

"Gosling here, sir," he said after taking a deep breath. "I'm afraid the subject had left only minutes before our arrival." He went on to explain what had happened and the gist of his questioning of Hogg's sister.

"Are you all fucking morons?" Zulu shouted down the line. "Start trawling the area. I'll get on to the Met and have them check all available cameras. I will authorise for every possible closed circuit camera in the country to be on the look-out for him. His picture will be above every screen. We *have* to find him, Gosling. It would be a shame if your career went no further forward." The line went dead.

"Miserable bastard," Gosling said aloud. His driver nodded in agreement. Whitehead was not a popular person within the department. Feared, maybe, but certainly not popular. Gosling opened the window and called to Carter, the man who had been watching from the back of his van.

"When we were in the house, did you manage to put a couple of bugs in there, Geoff?"

"Yes, Guv," he replied. "One in the living room stuck behind the wall mirror, one in the kitchen and one in her bedroom. She'll never spot them. There's also one in the phone." Gosling decided to pass on his chief's displeasure. If *he* was going to get a bollocking, so would his underlings.

"Right, well you can stay here in the van and listen in," he ordered. "I want to know everything that's said in that house." It was the way of the world; the dog bites the cat, the cat then bites the mouse. As for the mouse? He just got into the back of his van with a snarl and settled down, wedging his headphones in place.

Whitehead was as good as his word. In less than an hour, Hogg's photograph was on the dashboard of every police patrol car and nestling in the pockets of the very few policemen that still pounded the beat on foot. The sophisticated MI5 surveillance room had tapped in to almost every CCTV camera in the country. They had the necessary ability to do exactly that.

Just after two o'clock that afternoon, Hogg jumped down from the lorry in another service station at Scotch Corner on the A.1. main road. His driver was turning off there for the last leg of his run in to Middlesborough and told him that it was the best place to get another lift to where he wanted to be. He thanked the man, stretched and, the huge truck having moved off to continue it's journey, began to walk towards the cafe. As he did so, he noticed a police car entering the lorry park. The car, with only one officer on board, cruised slowly down the line of parked lorries towards him. Hogg ducked under one of the parked trailers and lay flat beside the gigantic rear wheels. The police car came to a halt beside the lorry he was under and, for a moment, he thought he had been spotted. The officer got out and walked up to the cab. Hogg had been unaware that a driver was sitting there.

"Alright, driver?" the policeman said. "Haven't picked up anyone from the London area, have you?" he enquired.

"Nah, mate," the gruff driver replied. "We ain't allowed to pick anyone up these days. New company policy. Who are you looking for anyway?"

"Some bloke from down in London. Been spying for the Ruskies apparently. A murderer as well." Hogg sucked in his breath at hearing this. So, they had told the police he had killed someone and was spying too. Then it dawned on him. They would probably be able to pin the death of Gary Briers on him. They wouldn't tell the police the real necessity for arresting him for obvious reasons. The policeman got back into his patrol car and moved slowly off. At that point, the engine of the truck started, smothering Hogg with blue-grey smoke and fumes. Trying to hold his breath yet choking at the same time, he rolled clear of the lorry before it moved. He walked quickly but cautiously over to the cafe and entered, buying a ham sandwich from the miserable looking woman behind the counter and stuffing it in his pocket. Moving to the toilets where one solitary man was relieving himself at the far end, Hogg did likewise then washed his hands and threw water over his face, rubbing it around his neck also. After the other man had left, he went into one of the cubicles, locking the door and sitting down to eat his sandwich. Unhygienic, he knew, but at least he could eat in peace, away from prying eyes. Replete from his snack, he drifted into a doze whilst still sitting on the toilet seat.

Someone laughing loudly outside the cubicle drew him back to the world of wakefulness. Stealing a look at his watch, he was surprised to find it was half past five. He left the toilets and went out of the cafe through a different door and into the car park. He stood near the door and surveyed the area before him. A short time later, an old, white Austin Allegro pulled in to the car park and two young men got out, locking the car behind them and moving towards the cafe. Hogg followed them in and watched from a distance. He was pleased to note that they had ordered a sit down meal rather than a take-away snack. That was all he needed to know; it would give him a little time. Leaving the cafe once more, he went straight to the Allegro. His universal key opened it easily and he slid behind the wheel, adjusted the seat for comfort and tried the key in the ignition. It turned and fired. Hogg drove the car out of the car park and emerged onto the A.1. heading north. He still had his mind set on Newcastle. There was someone there who he could call upon for help. Five miles further on however, his direction was changed for him.

As he passed junction fifty seven, a police car merged on to the motorway behind him. Ten seconds later, the rotating blue lights and siren came on as the patrol car raced up and sat almost on his rear bumper, the headlights flashing too. There was no way they could have known who was driving the car so the theft must have been discovered almost immediately. One of the young men had returned to the car to get his cigarettes and found it missing. The police were alerted and were on Hogg's tail. He dropped a gear and put his right foot to the floor. The ancient engine screamed in protest as he pushed the speedometer up to ninety five. He knew he had to get off the motorway or be caught so hurtled to the left at the next junction and then left again, passing a sign for Bishop Auckland. It meant nothing to Hogg. At the next roundabout, he went the wrong way round it and off to the right. The swerving, on-coming cars slowed his pursuer down considerably, giving him a little more headway. Having no idea where he was or even where he was heading, he threw the car into the first lane he came to on his left, the bodywork creaking under the strain and found himself in a narrow lane. Following the lane round to the left, he came to a major road and, with barely a glance for other traffic, turned right and found himself going towards somewhere called Consett. Surveying the rear view mirror, he was overjoyed to note the absence of any police vehicles or blue lights behind him. Not wanting to push his luck yet still wanting to get as far along as possible, he took another left turn in the direction of Wolsingham and continued for another twenty miles before going to the right. A much narrower road this time, after about five minutes he passed a group of houses bearing the name-plate of 'Dirt Pot'. The name gave him the first reason to smile in days. There was nothing to smile about after that, for just beyond the hamlet the tired old engine finally gave up and died in a cloud of blue smoke. Hogg free-wheeled to the right hand side and pulled up in front of a metal barred gate with fields full of sheep beyond. He had never in his life seen so many sheep.

It was just beginning to get darker now, the skies ahead of him turning a little greyer, approaching storm clouds scudding across the heavens. His watch made the time out to be eight o'clock. He turned and looked back at the way he had come, searching for any signs of pursuit and noticed the sun starting to set on the distant horizon, shades of pink, lilac and gold reflecting off the gathering clouds. Climbing over the gate, he set off across the countryside at a limping jog. With the undulating ground and occasional gorse bush, he would have somewhere to hide rather than be on the open road he had just left. Panting heavily, he came over a small rise in the ground and found the remains of a derelict cottage right in front of him. In the gathering darkness, he could just make out that the roof was completely missing and only the ancient brickwork of two walls remained along with a chimney stack. Hogg was shattered and so it would have to do; somewhere to rest up for a while, maybe for the night. He could hardly see in front of him now. There was a small alcove in one of the old walls that he surmised had been the fireplace in better days. He wedged himself into it and drew his knees up to his chin, wiping the sweat from his brow with his sleeve. He figured he had run for at least five miles. It was, in fact, only one and a half.

Two hours earlier, Roger Whitehead was sitting in his office, listening to a report from Paul Gosling.

"The description from the police up north fits our man, chief, even down to the clothes he was wearing. I've looked at the CCTV images they've sent across and I'm certain it's him," Gosling was telling him with some trepidation.

"How in the hell did he get all the way up to Scotch Corner without anyone seeing him?" Whitehead demanded, furiously tugging at his left ear lobe. It was a habit he had got in to whenever he was stressed. "I thought you had all the railway and coach stations covered. How did he get past you, for Christ's sake?"

"I can assure you, sir, that he did not use any of the main line or coach stations. They were all saturated."

"You had better get your team up there as quick as you can," Whitehead ordered after a brief pause for thought. "There will be a helicopter waiting for you at Battersea Heliport. While you are en route, make contact with a Sergeant Robson of Newcastle Police, I'll contact him and he will be expecting to hear from you. I'll send you a private number for him. The local police think he's an ordinary sergeant but he's actually attached to Special Branch. See if you can get some sort of lead on Hogg before morning. It's my bet that he's probably gone to ground for the night. Keep me informed of developments." The line went dead as Whitehead slammed the phone viciously back on to the cradle.

Less than half an hour later, Gosling and four others were airborne and heading north. He telephoned Sergeant Robson from his mobile on the number he had been given. Robson informed him that the stolen car had been found beside the road and gave him the location. The military twin rotor helicopter sped through the night sky, arriving over Weardale, just outside Ireshopeburn three hours later. Gosling looked down into the darkness as they hovered and saw blue lights flashing from three police cars forming a triangle on the ground. The huge aircraft hovered for a few moments, turned ninety degrees then started to descend slowly, coming to rest in the centre of the triangle. As the engine began to die down and the rotors slowed, Gosling and his men got out and, with heads bowed against the downdraught, hurried across to one of the cars where a man in jeans and a bomber jacket stood, smoking.

"Sergeant Robson?" Gosling enquired gruffly then, without waiting for an answer, continued, "I'm Gosling." He waved his well-worn I.D. card towards the other man. "What's the latest situation up here then?" Detective Sergeant John Robson glanced fleetingly at the wallet being waved in his face and sniffed loudly, wiping his nose with the back of his hand. At forty one, he had been in the force for twenty years, the last eight as an undercover operative for Special Branch. Police stations in all of the major cities had at least one S.B. officer in their midst without knowing it, usually a sergeant or above, undercover. Robson was over six foot tall with broad shoulders, slightly balding at the front but his jet black hair swept back at the sides. One look at him and you automatically knew he was not the sort of person that you went up against. He had dealt with these London spooks before, six years previously when a Russian submarine had been spotted off the Farne Islands. They had been next to useless then and he did not have high expectations of them now either. Blowing a smoke ring into the air, he flicked his cigarette away in to the darkness where it disappeared into the long grass.

"It seems your man dumped the stolen car on the B6295 then went over a gate in to some fields," he said, matter-of-factly. "The police dog picked up his scent and he appeared to be heading north-east towards Hangman Hill. Trouble is, the dog lost the scent because of all the bastard sheep around. Thousands of them it seems. The dog handler's gone off now; no sense in him hanging around."

Gosling instructed his team to split up into two of the cars and walked quickly with Robson to the third car, levering himself into the front passenger seat. Robson, sniffing again, resigned himself to the back seat. The convoy, with Gosling in the lead, set off from the field and crunched across gravel before merging on to the roadway.

"For fuck sake kill those blue lights, will you?" Gosling snarled. "Otherwise we may as well have sirens blasting as well, really let him know we're coming." Robson relayed the order to the other two cars and the lights were extinguished immediately. "Have you called in a chopper with a heat-seeking camera?" Gosling asked, without much hope. The answer surprised him.

"We've only got the one up here," Robson replied indignantly. "It's just finished refuelling and on it's way here from Morpeth." Gosling shook his head slowly. These bloody provincials, he thought to himself.

A few minutes later, they came to the spot where Hogg had decamped from the stolen car, leaving it with it's nose almost buried into the gate. Another two patrol cars were parked beside and behind it. As the men got out of their three cars, the steady throb of the police chopper could be heard approaching from the west. Everyone looked up and saw the blinking, yellow anti-collision light stabbing the dark night sky. The experienced pursuit crew had already been briefed before take-off and knew what was expected of them and what to look for. The aircraft banked away and slowed right down as it headed away from them at a height of just over two hundred feet, it's powerful searchlight sweeping slowly to the left and then right on the ground ahead.

"Come on then you slovenly bunch," Gosling shouted, climbing the gate, "look lively. I want to be there when they catch up with the bastard." Sergeant Robson started to follow suit but was stopped by Gosling. "No need for you to get your nice clean shoes dirty, Sergeant," he said firmly, placing a large, firm hand on the man's chest. He did not want the local police hanging around when he caught up with his quarry, even if he *was* Special Branch. Only Gosling knew that the only way the wanted man was coming back would be in a zipped up body-bag, ready for the morgue. Gosling and his team set off at a steady trot in the direction the chopper had taken, playing their flash-lights low on the ground in front of them.

Hogg awoke from his fitful slumber as soon as he heard the helicopter's engine in the distance. He scrambled over some fallen bricks and cautiously peered over what remained of one wall. He clearly saw the police aircraft and its searchlight sweeping from side to side as it came nearer to his haven. Knowing that they would probably be equipped with a heat-seeking, night vision camera that would pick up the heat from his body, he hurried back to the fireplace and managed to work his way a couple of feet up the chimney stack. With his back to one wall of the chimney and his feet pressed against the other, he held himself there. A few moments later, he saw the light from the chopper probing the ruins of the cottage and could feel the wind from the rotors as it hovered overhead. After what seemed like hours but was in fact only minutes, the aircraft moved slowly away again on the same course. As the throbbing sound of the engine subsided, Hogg lowered himself, crept from his hiding place and chanced a look over the wall once more. He could see the flashing amber light gradually moving away from him. Just as he thought he had outwitted them, he heard voices coming from the opposite direction and turned to face this new threat. With their torches bobbing as they ran, Gosling and his team were approaching the ruins, now only a couple of hundred yards away. Hogg knew he would not survive a closer inspection of the cottage and so slipped over the wall, heading off to one side at an angle, taking care not to make any noise or stumble. He came to a slight dip in the ground and all but fell into it, landing on his hands and knees. The beam from one of the powerful torches played over his head, missing him in the dip and then turned away. He peered back over the lip and saw their flash-lights weaving in and out of the derelict cottage that had been his hiding place. A few minutes later the lights continued on their previous heading, the same direction that the helicopter had taken shortly before. The fugitive breathed a sigh of relief and rested his weary head on his arms.

He set off at a tangent and headed across more fields in the dark, often stumbling in to ditches and flocks of sheep who scattered as he approached them. He had no idea of his direction now, but carried on regardless. His ankle, which *had* started to heal, was beginning to throb a little more, making his headway slower than he would have liked. He came across the occasional ruins and, now and then, a farmhouse, giving these a wide berth. The risk of causing some farmyard dog to start barking was too great for him to chance. The cold and the dampness of the earth was eating in to him now and hunger had started to set in. At one point he sat down to rest with his back against an old tree that swayed and groaned like some arthritic giant in the chilly wind that swept across the bleak moors. Then he was up and running again.

By a little after five in the morning, just before dawn, he came across a small hamlet by the name of Catton. Hogg cautiously approached the first house he came to, set back from the road behind a short row of conifer trees. There was no sign of life from within the white-walled cottage and he crept up the drive, keeping to the grass verge to lessen any noise. An old Ford car sat on the driveway facing out and it took him mere seconds to get the door open. He found one of his many keys fitted the ignition and he turned it to disengage the steering lock. Releasing the handbrake, he allowed the car to roll down the slope to the road and turned it to face downhill, climbing into the seat as it went. Less than a hundred yards further, the road levelled out and the car came to a halt. Hogg turned the key all the way and fired up the engine without revving it too much, although he felt he was far enough away from the house not to be heard. Driving off, he passed imposing Langley Castle on his left and entered Haydon Bridge, turned right on to the main road and followed the signs for Newcastle. Less than half an hour later he was in the city itself and pulled in to the kerb behind a stationary taxi. He took directions from the sleepy driver and found the address he was seeking in Bentinck Street.

* * *

Scott Goodman had been his cell-mate for a time when he had been in Pentonville Prison years earlier and Hogg hoped and prayed that the man still lived there. In case the car was spotted by a passing police patrol, having been reported stolen, he drove a quarter of a mile away, left it in a small car park adjacent to a corner shop and walked back to Goodman's house. It was now six thirty. He decided he had no option but to try the doorbell. It sounded from far within the house and a dog barked momentarily. Receiving no response from the bell, he tried again and kept his finger on the button for a full five seconds. The dog started barking again and this time continued to do so. Then came the sound of someone coming down the stairs, swearing and cursing loudly. The heavily accented voice sounded like Goodman but, to Hogg, all these Geordies sounded the same. The door opened on a chain and Scott Goodman peered through the narrow gap, his puffy eyes full of sleep.

"Scott?" Hogg ventured tentatively. "It's me, Jim, ….. Jimmy Hogg." Goodman rubbed his eyes fiercely with both hands and squinted at him some more before recognition eventually showed on his face.

"Fookin' hell," he exclaimed at last. "D'ye nah what bliddy time it is, man?"

"Yeah, time you opened the fucking door and let me in. Old Bill's on my tail and I'm a bit on the desperate side, mate." The chain came off and the door swung wide as Hogg stepped over the threshold, pushing the door shut behind him. He followed Goodman through to the kitchen at the back of the two up, two down terraced house. Scott's wife had done a runner during his last holiday at Her Majesty's pleasure and it showed. Empty lager cans littered the rusting, metal draining board of the sink which was filled completely with mugs, plates and a grimy, grunge ridden saucepan. The huge, red, plastic ashtray, almost hidden by crushed, empty cans, was full to overflowing with cigarette butts and ash, and there were signs that Goodman existed solely on takeaways judging by the number of pizza boxes and chop suey cartons that spilled from the filthy, swing top plastic rubbish bin. The scruffy dog that had been barking came in to the room and, after a quick sniff at Hogg's feet and crotch, began to hunt round the kitchen, presumably in a vain search for food. Goodman weighed the kettle in his hand and, satisfied that it contained sufficient water, switched it on. He pulled two dirty mugs from the sink and rinsed them under the cold water tap. He spooned in some instant coffee, still yawning and sat down to wait for the kettle to boil.

"Ye had best tell me what all this is aboot, Jimmy man" he said, rubbing his face with both hands, his stubble making a rasping sound on his palms as he did so. So Hogg told him, right from the beginning, everything that had transpired from the burglary right up to the present time. Goodman said nothing, just listened and poured steaming water into the two mugs.

"....... they've been following every move on cameras and now they're putting it about that I'm a spy for the Russians *and* a fucking murderer as well, for Christ's sake," Hogg concluded with exasperation.

"Alreet, ye can hole up here for a few days," Goodman told him, lighting a roll-up. "but I'm a bit short of cash for food, ye nah."

"Don't worry, mate," Hogg said with a grin. "I've got a few quid." He peeled off five twenty pound notes and handed them over. "That should keep us going for a while. I'll be out of your hair as soon as I can get something sorted out." Goodman took the money eagerly and without hesitation, noting with glee the wad of cash that Hogg put back in his pocket.

"Aye, well I'm gannin' to the shop to get some grub and the papers," he smiled, struggling into a pair of well-worn, once white but now stained grey trainers. He went out of the house, leaving Hogg alone with his thoughts except for the ragged old dog which sat in front of him, staring at him. He looked at his watch. Seven forty five in the morning. So much had happened in such a short time, he felt completely worn out, having had no sleep since dozing in the lorry along the motorway the previous morning. Going through to the front room, the story was much the same there. The small two seater sofa was shining with dog hair and the only armchair had long since seen better days, the stuffing filtering out of one of the arms. He plumped for the chair as it seemed the lesser of the two evils and sank back into it gratefully. He was so tired, he felt he could not even string two words together, let alone a complete sentence.

At around the same moment in time, Paul Gosling was speaking to Whitehead on his coded mobile phone. He and his team had reached Haydon Bridge and were resting in a cafe with coffee and bacon sandwiches.

"He's got to be in the area somewhere, Gosling," Whitehead shouted down the line. "Stay where you are while I delve a bit deeper, see if he has any known contacts up there. He wouldn't have made that journey up North for no good reason." The line went dead and Gosling pulled a face. As he picked up his sandwich, his phone rang again. Answering the call, he heard Sergeant Robson's voice.

"A car was stolen from Catton, not far from where he was last seen. That sort of thing doesn't happen out there so it's probably your man," Robson informed him. "I've circulated details of Hogg as well as the car and just hope it gets spotted on one of the cameras."

"Make sure you keep me up to date with developments," Gosling ordered him and switched off. He had only just filled his mouth with more of the sandwich when his phone buzzed. He angrily wiped grease from his chin with a paper serviette and answered it. It was Whitehead.

"Hogg was in Pentonville prison with a Scott Anthony Goodman and his last known address, according to his Probation Officer was in Newcastle." He gave the address and Gosling wrote it down.

"I'll get on to it, Chief," he said, standing up abruptly and pushing the wooden chair noisily back across the linoleum floor with his legs. The rest of his squad were none too happy about leaving their breakfasts and took the remains of their sandwiches with them, following Gosling out to the car that Robson had supplied for their use. As they entered the main road, Robson called again.

"That car that was stolen Catton that I told you about. It's turned up abandoned in a back street in Newcastle."

"Was it anywhere near Bentinck Street, by any chance?" Gosling asked hopefully, remembering the address he had received from Whitehead.

"Funny you should say that. About a five minute walk away from it," Robson replied. "How did you know that?"

"Never mind," Gosling sighed. "Just keep an eye on it from a distance and meet me there, alright? I think I might know where to find our man." Without waiting for a reply he switched off and sat back in the front passenger seat. "Looks like we may be on, boys," he said with a wry smile and pulled his service revolver from his shoulder holster and checked it. This was an unnecessary action as Gosling had checked it a dozen or more times in the past couple of hours from force of habit. He was looking forward to catching up with his quarry at last.

The front door closing awoke Hogg with a start and, for just a moment, he did not know where he was. It seemed as if he had only just closed his eyes but when he looked down at his watch, he found to his amazement that almost an hour had passed since his old friend had gone out. Goodman had returned with fresh milk, two spaghetti bolognese ready meals, eight cans of strong lager and some newspapers. He also reeked from the smell of stale beer and had obviously had a few quick refresher bottles from the local off-licence on the way back.

"Anything in the papers?" Hogg asked, rubbing his eyes and yawning before sitting down on the kitchen chair.

"Why aye, ye're fookin' famous, man," Scott replied with a grin. He threw the two papers on to Hogg's lap and went out to the kitchen.

The death of Diana was still the front page news but on pages four and five was the article about a known cat-burglar who had been selling stolen secrets to a foreign power. No mention was made of the Russians but it was certainly inferred. He had apparently stolen the secret documents from the house of a senior MI5 man whose house he had burgled. The story went on to say that he, Hogg, had then shot and killed a newspaper reporter on some waste land behind the Bull and Bush public house near Hampstead after he had been followed by the journalist. There were two unnamed witnesses to this murder too. The article was accompanied by a photograph of

Hogg, a still from video footage from the service station at Scotch Corner. Beside the large photo was a smaller picture of Gary Briers, the murder victim, smiling with his wife on a holiday. Hogg quickly read through the whole story then sank back in despair.

"This is all bollocks, Scott!" he shouted out. Goodman came back into the room with steaming plates, fresh from the rust encrusted microwave oven.

"Aye, I nah that, Jim man," he said with a nod. "The bastards are stitchin' ye up good an' proper. They won't stop at anything to catch ye."

Hogg stabbed his fork into the food whilst sitting in the armchair and ate greedily for he was ravenous, not having eaten since the previous afternoon. They both remained silent while the food was eaten. Goodman looked as though he hadn't had a good meal for some time either. Finally, Hogg slid his empty plate on to the small table beside the chair, belched loudly and then sighed, sinking back into the chair.

"I don't really know what to do, Scott," he said at length. "I came up here to get away from it all and they've found me again, it seems. Right now I think my only chance is to get out of the country as soon as I can. I've been told of a bloke down in Folkestone who's got a fishing boat. He might be able to get me across the channel. I might give that a try.

"Trouble is," Scott replied, "with all this CCTV everywhere they can find ye easily and they've even got the polis on t'ye."

"I know," Hogg muttered, rubbing his hands across his face. "I'm bloody knackered, mate. I can't even think straight at the moment."

"Get yeself oopstairs and have a lie doon, man," his friend told him. "Ye'll feel better after a bit of a kip." Hogg nodded and trudged wearily up to the dingy bedroom. Kicking off his shoes, he flopped down on to the lumpy mattress and closed his eyes but sleep eluded him despite his tiredness. There was too much to worry about, not least the thought of just staying alive. He sat up and put his feet back on the floor, his head in his hands and slipped his shoes back on. The sound of a mobile phone ringing downstairs brought his keen senses back and he went to the door and listened. There was just a whispering from below so he gently opened the bedroom door and went out on to the landing and leaned over the bannister rail. He

68

could just make out Goodman's voice.

"Aye, he's here noo. This goes against everything I was brought up with, but I divven want nae more trooble, Mister Robson," he heard Scott saying softly. "I can't go back inside and do another stretch, ye nah. I've been straight fer a while now." There was silence for a few moments as Scott was obviously listening to the caller then he spoke again. "Well alright. I'll open the front door for ye an' leave it on the catch then I'll go oot the back so I'm not here when ye all come in, but give me a few minutes to get clear." Hogg heard the faint bleep as the phone was switched off. He crept down the stairs and, as Goodman came out into the hall, Hogg punched him hard, catching him on his left cheekbone and sending him sprawling.

"You fucking bastard grass," he yelled, spittle running over his chin. "You're supposed to be my fucking mate."

"They know ye're here, Jim," Goodman whimpered, a huge red mark starting to well up beneath his eye. "The copper who called me knows me from way back and said he'd fit me up with something good and proper if I didn't help. He'd do it, an' all." Hogg gave the cowering man a swift kick to the ribs and headed for the back door. Outside was a small yard bounded by a rickety six foot fence. One look at the gate and the weeds growing high in front of it told him that it hadn't been opened for many a year so he scrambled over the rotting wood and landed in a cobbled alley behind the house. Another alleyway ran off at right angles and he fled into it, his legs pounding like pistons. Within seconds he reached another road and ran along it as fast as he could manage with his injury. Coming to a stop at a main road, he saw a bus coming to a halt at a stop about a hundred yards away and sprinted for it, his ankle starting to burn like hell. The destination board on the bus showed it was going to Hexham so he paid the fare to the end and settled down halfway along the bus, sliding as far down in the seat as he could without raising too much suspicion. He had no idea of where Hexham was but anywhere that got him away from the area was good enough for him.

The ageing bus pulled away with a shudder of its tired diesel engine as it gathered speed. Only about a mile farther on, Hogg noticed a car for sale in the front garden of a house as they passed.

Two hundred and fifty pounds, said the sign in the windscreen. Alighting at the next stop, he ran back and knocked at the door. An extremely overweight man wearing a baseball cap, T-shirt and jeans answered his knock, his eyebrows knitted together in a questioning manner.

"I'll give you two hundred cash for the car," Hogg said with a smile, hooking his thumb over his shoulder towards the old Toyota. The man looked him up and down, appraising him before responding.

"Two twenty an' yer can have the keys," he said, taking them from a shelf inside the door and dangling them in the air.

"Okay, as long as I can have your hat as well," Hogg told him. The man was taken aback at this suggestion but happily swept it from his head and held it out. Hogg took it and handed over the money, the man's greedy eyes ogling the wad of cash as it was counted out into his hands.

"I'll need yer name an' address fer the log book," he said. Hogg plucked a name from thin air and also gave an imaginary address in York. The man appeared to be satisfied and Hogg unlocked the car and started the engine. It made a loud, rattling noise as it did so. He winced slightly at the sound and crunched the car into gear, gradually edging out across the pavement and into the traffic. He turned to his left, away from Goodman's house and increased speed to thirty until he found a petrol station and pulled in as the fuel light had come on as soon as he had started the engine. He put the scruffy flat cap on his head, pulled the peak down as low over his face as he could and got out of the car. Hunched over, he filled the tank and went inside to pay. He simply handed over the notes, turned and left without a word. Hogg didn't want to be in view of any cameras that may be about for any longer than was necessary. A few miles more brought him to the motorway that led back down South and, once on it, he increased his speed to seventy, blending in with the other traffic.

Hogg drove at a steady speed for hours until, just outside Peterborough, he felt he had to stop, get something to eat and rest for a short time and so left the motorway, following signs to Yaxley. Within a few miles he came to the town. Pulling up outside the first general store he came to, Hogg got out and stretched his arms and legs. It was only then, breathing in the fresh air, that he realised he had been inhaling exhaust fumes for the past few hours. Letting the old engine cool down for a while seemed a good idea and he went into the shop and purchased a couple of sausage rolls, a newspaper and a bottle of Orangina to quench his thirst. He sat back in the car in the parking spot opposite the shop, munching on one of the savoury snacks and taking a long swallow of the orange drink before unfolding the paper and scanning it quickly. The story of himself was on page five and he read it right through, then read it again. It seemed that the authorities were able to track him through various cameras that they could tap in to which was how they had traced him so easily. He finished off the sugary drink and drove further along the road until he came to a quiet spot next to a bowling green. He wound the seat down a little and closed his eyes for a moment. Just resting them for that few minutes felt so good. That few minutes turned into hours.

* * * *

Roger Whitehead studied the map pinned to the wall of his office, mentally making his way between the different coloured pins attached to it. His quarry had somehow made good his escape from his sister's house and made his way North. He tried to put himself in to the mind of the man he was chasing. The only connection he could find was Scott Goodman who had shared a cell with Hogg for a time, but Goodman was only a small time rogue, hardly big enough to be of any practical help to Hogg. The telephone on his desk began to ring.

"Gosling here, Chief," he heard down the line. "When we went in through the front door, Goodman was lying on the floor with a broken nose and a black eye. Our man overheard him on the phone to Sergeant Robson and disappeared only minutes before we went in." Whitehead sank back in his maroon leather chair in exasperation, banging his clenched fist forcefully onto the desk. "I think we should wait around here until we get further info. At the moment, without a lead we've got nowhere to go." Whitehead was inclined to agree with him and said that he would have every camera in the area put on high alert in an attempt to locate the fugitive. He switched off the telephone and sat back, his fingertips together, elbows at his side and closed his eyes to concentrate. What would he do in Hogg's position? The man had narrowly avoided being caught at the house in Newcastle and must know that he was being tracked and possibly

71

by cameras as well as intelligence sources. His next move now must surely be to head back down South where he had more contacts who may be able to assist him, areas that he knew well. He called Gosling.

"Let's take a chance that he's headed back this way," he told the man. "Get back on the chopper and make your way down here. At the moment, there's no particular hurry until we can locate him again."

When Hogg awoke from his slumber in the car it was dark. His watch showed eleven forty. He got out of the car and relieved himself against a wooden fence. Sitting back behind the wheel he figured he could make Central London by two in the morning. He turned the ignition key and, to his amazement, the ancient Toyota started immediately. Back-tracking, he found his way back to the motorway and gradually pushed the car up to just over seventy. He figured that any police cruiser that spotted a car doing just a few miles an hour over the limit would ignore him. He was right. Without incident and at a steady pace he arrived in Soho at a quarter past two and parked just off Soho Square. He walked through to Silk's, a clip-joint in Great Windmill Street and found his old friend Alan Randall standing on the door.

"How's it going, Al?" he asked, leaning against the wall. Randall immediately grabbed him by his jacket collar and roughly tugged him inside the entrance, pushing him through the beaded curtain and into the bar area, glancing both ways along the street as he did so.

"Fuck me, Jimmy!" he exclaimed, releasing his strong grip. "Old Bill's got your card well and truly marked, my son. They've been plotting up all over Soho looking for you for the past couple of days, asking all sorts of questions from everyone. Causing a right balls up for us all, they are"

"It's not true what they're saying about me in the papers, Al" Hogg informed him. "They're trying to fit me up because of what I know, that thing I was telling you about in Bar Italia?"

"Yeah, I'd figured that out, mate, but you can't dwell in Central London, Jim. Too many people are looking for you and there are more grasses on the streets than enough, you know that. All looking to make a nice few quid from the police in exchange for a quick phone call."

"Well, I'm going to try to get out of the country for a while until things die down a bit," Hogg replied. "I've got a plan of sorts in my head."

"Don't tell me about it, Jim, I don't want to know," was Randall's response. "The less you tell anyone the safer you'll be. Just get yourself going. I don't fancy having *my* collar felt as well."

"Okay, Alan. Thanks for the tip anyway. Be seeing you."

"I certainly hope so," Randall said, half to himself as Hogg went out through the curtain and in to the street.

"One of your friends, Alan?" asked Samantha, one of the club's scantily dressed hostesses who was lounging on the red leather sofa just inside the door. Her long black hair swayed as she turned to look up at him.

"No," he lied convincingly. "Just some mug chancer trying to do a bit of business, is all." He sincerely hoped Hogg would make it to safety. He had known the man for many years, since their schooldays in fact and, though they seldom now met, quite liked him for all his faults.

Hogg returned to his car and headed out through South London and picked up the motorway for the coast. He just hoped and prayed that he could find the boat that Briers had told him about. Leaving the motorway at junction thirteen, he followed the signs for Folkestone Harbour and pulled up in the car park of the dilapidated Burstin Hotel beside the waterfront shortly before five in the morning. Hogg surveyed himself in the rear-view mirror. He badly needed a shave and his hair was all over the place. A good wash wouldn't go amiss either. He then realised that the change in his normal appearance might go in his favour and with his fingers, rumpled his hair even more.

He got out and walked back, turning under an old railway bridge behind a pub and found the outer harbour on his right. He could make out some boats gently swaying on the out-going tide and guessed that they would soon be high and dry when the sea water had abated. It was too dim to make out any names on the boats so he approached a man who had just rowed a small tender to the slip-way.

"Has the Joanne-Marie come in yet, mate?" he asked with a smile. The man eyed him cautiously for a moment before deciding to reply as he tied his small craft to a bollard on the quayside.

73

"You'll be wanting Ted Jarvis," the man said, nodding wisely. "He's still out. Won't be back in now afore the basin's dry so he'll probably stay out until late this afternoon now if I know him." Hogg thanked him and walked away, finding an early opening cafe just inside Tontine Street. He went in and treated himself to a full fried breakfast which he devoured greedily. At eight o'clock he wandered round the corner and found a bed and breakfast guest house. The place looked run down with once white paint flaking from the walls and desperately needed a complete refurbishment but it suited his purpose and the hand-written sign in the window told him there were vacancies within. He prodded the bell with his finger and, after a few moments the door opened. An overweight man in his fifties with long, wavy, sandy hair gazed down the steps at him and pursed his lips unnecessarily. Hogg booked him for an iron hoof.

"Can I help you, sir?" the man enquired, fluttering his eyelashes.

"I'm looking for a room and I see you've got vacancies," Hogg stated, inclining his head toward the sign.

"Of course. Won't you come inside?" the proprietor said, stepping back and holding the door open wide for Hogg to enter. A small bureau stood in the hallway and Hogg was asked to enter his name and address in the visitor's book. He stuck up a false one and was shown to a small room on the second floor having paid his twenty pounds. "Do you have any luggage at all?" he was asked.

"No mate," Hogg retorted. "I'm only getting a few hours kip because my car's broken down and won't be ready until this afternoon. Any chance of giving me a knock around mid-day?"

"Certainly, sir," the ginger replied with a sickly smile. "I can do that for you." He went out with Hogg's cash nestling in his pocket, closing the door softly behind him. Hogg looked around the room. A single bed, well used, a small wardrobe and an upright wooden chair in front of the window. With no lock on the door, he wedged the back of the chair under the handle. It wouldn't stop a determined intruder but it would give him extra time to get out of the window and make his way to the ground. The room was sufficient for his needs. Kicking off his shoes, he sank back on to the bed fully clothed and was immediately asleep. Throughout the morning he kept waking briefly with a start after continuous vivid dreams in which he was being chased through dark tunnels by Gary Briers with a big, gaping hole in his forehead. Every time he looked back, the hole had got bigger until he could actually see through to the other side of the man's head. He could see the tunnel stretching out before him for miles and miles and Briers was gaining on him with every step. Each time he felt the hand on his shoulder he awoke, sweating despite the chill in the room.

That same morning, as Hogg was settling back on his bed, Whitehead called Gosling once again.

"I've asked Robson to go back to Goodman and have another word with him, lean on him a bit more" he informed his enforcer. "I'm certain that Hogg has told him more than he's letting on."

"Okay, Chief," Gosling replied with a weary sigh. "Once he's had another go at him, we'll see what he comes up with." It didn't take Sergeant Robson very long to obtain the information that he required. Scott Goodman was not a brave man, but he was a sensible one who valued his liberty. Robson immediately called Whitehead with the details of Hogg's plan to locate the fishing boat in Folkestone, although the name of the boat was unknown.

"Right, about time," Whitehead snarled when he heard the news.

"We're on our way, Chief," Gosling said when Whitehead gave him the information. "We'll land at Lydd Airport which is near to Folkestone and await any further information." Whitehead grimaced at the informal salutation from Gosling and threw his phone back on to his desk, muttering under his breath.

Hogg was awake again when he was startled by the loud knock on his door. He rolled out of the uncomfortable bed and opened it to find his host, still smiling, telling him that it was just after twelve o'clock and asking if he would like some tea or coffee. Hogg decided on the coffee. He needed to be alert that afternoon. Half an hour later he was making his way out of the front door having been shaken limply by the hand. It took him just five minutes to walk to the harbour and immediately found the boat he was seeking tied up at the slipway. A wiry man in his late fifties was manhandling two boxes over the side on to the concrete apron. Hogg sidled up to the man.

"Are you Ted?" he asked.

"That's me, son," came the reply. The man continued with his task without even looking up.

"Gary Briers told me to come and see you, said you'd be able to help me." The sailor stopped in mid-lift but didn't even look up at him. After a few seconds, he slowly placed the wooden crate onto the ground.

"You must be fucking mad," he hissed in a fierce whisper, glaring at Hogg.

"Look, mate," Hogg said quickly. "I'm desperate and Gary said you'd be okay with getting me across the Channel to France. I've got a grand in cash up front," he said with a nod, patting his pocket. The man studied Hogg for a moment then appeared to make his mind up.

"Get on board and sit down on the deck in corner of the wheelhouse," he ordered. "We'll get under way while we still have the water." He left the boxes on the quayside. "But for Christ's sake keep out of sight." Hogg lifted his leg over the rail and went inside, sitting on the wooden deck with his back against one wall in the corner. Five minutes later, Jarvis entered and started the ancient diesel engine. Without a glance at his passenger, he went back out and cast off the ropes holding the old vessel to the shore then returned and pushed the throttle while spinning the wheel. Within minutes they were rolling out of the harbour entrance and Hogg felt the swell of the sea, lifting and dropping the boat as they pitched forward into ever deeper water. Jarvis unhooked the microphone and called up the Coastguard to inform them that he was on his way out for another haul and would be back around eight that evening. He looked down at Hogg who was still wedged tightly in the corner.

"Have to let them know I'm going out again or they'll get suspicious," he said. "Two and a half hours and we'll have you in Audreselles, halfway between Boulogne and Calais. It's a tiny fishing village, no customs or anyone official. From there, you're on your own. You got the cash?" Hogg rummaged in his pocket and counted out one thousand pounds, handing it up to Jarvis who had counted it at the same time. He stuffed it into the inside pocket of his reefer coat and turned his attention to his GPS screen.

At around the same time, Paul Gosling took a call from Whitehead as he was finishing his second mug of coffee in the staff canteen at Lydd Airport in Kent.

"Had a call from the Coastguard at Dover," Whitehead informed him. "It appears that a fishing boat from Folkestone is doing something rather out of character. Gone out again almost as soon as he arrived back in the harbour. Coastguard were suspicious enough to alert us. I had asked them to keep an eye out for anything out of the ordinary. Get yourself airborne again and take a look. The boat is called the Joanne-Marie and I'll give you it's latest position and heading." Gosling scribbled down the figures in his notebook and broke the connection, calling to his team as he did so. Going out on to the tarmac they found the bright yellow RAF search and rescue helicopter standing a hundred yards away, the three man crew chatting idly in the doorway. Gosling approached the pilot and handed him the coordinates Whitehead had given him. His team, complete with weapons bags climbed in behind him. Within minutes the huge machine was lifting into the air, the noise drowning out any attempt at conversation. The winch-man handed Gosling a headset so that he was able to communicate with the pilot. Very soon afterwards the pilot's voice came through the earpiece.

"I think that's your target, about two miles ahead of us now, on a heading of one seven two degrees," he said, matter-of-factly. Gosling went forward into the cockpit and, steadying himself on the backs of the seats, leaned between the pilot and his colleague. He saw a small, blue and white fishing boat moving quite quickly across the South West sea lane. The pilot gradually brought his craft down to a little over a hundred feet above the choppy water and closed on the boat, decreasing speed at the same time.

Hogg was still seated on the deck with his back against the shuddering wall when he saw the giant helicopter bearing down upon them.

"What the fuck is *that*?" he yelled, pointing. Jarvis turned and looked in the direction Hogg had indicated. The blood drained from his face in an instant.

"Jeeesus," he muttered, half to himself and then, out loud, "It's the RAF rescue chopper. They're usually only around if there's been a Mayday call and I ain't heard one so they must be looking for *you*, son."

The big yellow aircraft was alongside them now and Hogg could clearly see a man in the open doorway bringing binoculars up to his eyes. He scurried on all fours to the other side of the cabin in an attempt to stay out of view. The radio crackled into life and a tinny

77

voice came through the speaker.

"Joanne-Marie this is Rescue Four. Maintain your current heading and slow to half speed, please. I will be winching an officer down on to your aft deck, understood?" Jarvis understood alright but had no intention of complying. He swung the wheel hard to the right, almost reversing his course. The old boat listed sharply, groaning in protestation at this extra abnormal strain it was being put under.

"Bollocks to that!" Jarvis exclaimed. "I'm not going to get myself nicked just for a bit of cash."

"What are you doing?" Hogg screamed at the top of his voice. "If we go back they'll kill me and you as well."

"Not me, mate. I'll just tell 'em you hired me to take you out. Don't know nothing about anything, me."

"Don't you see?" Hogg pleaded. "They won't want to leave any witnesses so you'll have to be killed as well." The wily old skipper wasn't paying any heed to Hogg's whining and was heading at full speed for the closest piece of land he could see, the old boat rocking and heaving.

"I'm going to run ashore at Dungeness," he said, his weathered eyes squinting into the distance at the barren stretch of shingle beach they were heading towards. "You can jump off there and take your chances."

Just then, the rear window shattered with a huge bang as a heavy calibre bullet went through it and blasted into the control panel. At the same time, the rattle of a light machine pistol opened up putting shells through the roof. Hogg felt his bowels start to loosen and only just managed to control himself. Jarvis stumbled to one side and let out a string of obscenities. A side window exploded and Jarvis was thrown across the cabin by the force of the bullet that hit him in the middle of his chest. Dead before he hit the decking, he lay crumpled on his back, his unseeing eyes wide as if in disbelief, gazing at the holes in the roof of the rickety wheelhouse.

By now, tears were streaming down Hogg's trembling cheeks as he chanced a look over the edge and saw the beach coming to meet him at a rapid pace. He held on tight to the wheel and braced himself for the impact which, when it came, was surprisingly softer than he had imagined it would be. There was a grinding sound as the keel of the fishing boat ran aground on to the shingle and swiftly came to a halt, it's bow pointing skywards. Hogg was thrown forward and received a painful blow to his upper chest from the spoked wooden wheel. Quickly clambering through the smashed windscreen and over the bow, he landed on the stony beach. The helicopter swooped low and fast overhead and, as he started to run, three more shots were fired in quick succession, kicking up pebbles and sand a foot or two to his right and in front. Tucking his head down, he ran for his life as the helicopter slowly descended to the beach some two hundred yards behind him. Due to its size, the pilot could not land the machine too quickly and this gave Hogg a little headway.

Just over a hundred yards ahead of him, he saw a white refrigerated van pull up in the car park of The Pilot public house. The elderly driver, wearing a far from white coat got out, leaving the diesel engine running and went round to the back doors which he opened wide, drawing out a large tray of fresh fish. With the tray in his hand, he looked on in wonderment as his vehicle suddenly pulled away from him at speed with Hogg behind the wheel. The driver stood open-mouthed for almost a minute, watching his van disappear into the distance down the long, straight coast road, unable to comprehend what had just happened.

Two men carrying long barrelled sniper rifles arrived at his side, panting. They looked along the road in the direction Hogg had taken, turned and ran back towards the beach. Less than a minute later, the huge helicopter rose noisily into the air once more, the nose dipping as it moved forward. The van driver watched all this happen, his lower jaw almost on his chest, the tray of fish still held close to his waist but now sloping slightly down so that three of the fish fell to the tarmac of the car park with a loud slapping sound. He slowly turned back to face the road once again, watching the helicopter dip lower. His van was no longer in sight.

Hogg had got the old vehicle up to a little over seventy miles an hour, overtaking a saloon car that was poodling along behind a bus at the legal speed limit of forty. He saw a sign for Romney Sands Caravan Park on his left and, on a whim, spun the wheel to turn into the park. The wheels rumbled as he went over the miniature steam railway track and he turned first right, coming to a halt beside one of the older caravans. Switching off the engine, he looked out and up just as the helicopter flew across him, following the course of the road. He listened intently and heard the sound of the beating rotors gradually disappear into the distance. The sound told him that they had not come down to land and were moving further away from him having missed seeing him make the turn. It gave him the opportunity he needed to elude them.

Walking back round towards the entrance, he found a small station and was overjoyed to note that one of the steam engines was just pulling in to the station with its train of carriages trundling along behind it. Hogg walked nonchalantly along the platform, slid open one of the miniature carriage doors and, ducking down to enter, sat himself down inside. After what seemed an age but was in fact only a minute or so, the train started to slowly move out of the station. Moving between the fields on one side and some houses on the other, he studied the route of the railway that was displayed on the inside wall of the carriage. The names of the up-coming stops meant nothing to him but he noted that the journey terminated at Hythe. The first station they reached was New Romney and then the train took a gradual left sweep towards a main road. Then it happened. The helicopter unexpectedly appeared alongside the train, travelling at the same speed, no more than a hundred feet above the ground. Hogg almost burst into tears when he saw one of the men looking directly at him through high-powered binoculars. It then suddenly increased speed and Hogg leaned out of the open window and gazed on in dismay as he watched it descend in the far distance ahead of the train. They would be waiting for him at the next station, Jefferstone Lane. There was only one way out. Even at the train's relatively slow speed of about twenty five miles an hour, he knew he would have to be cautious. He slid the door open and, judging his moment carefully, launched himself from the carriage. He landed on his good foot and rolled several times in long grass before coming to a halt on his side. A few passengers noticed him from the passing carriages but he ignored their stares. After the train had passed he got up, slightly winded and made his way through the long, wind-swept grass and between grazing sheep, heading towards the main road they had passed beneath only a minute before.

On reaching the main coast road, he found a bus stop less than a hundred yards away and walked quickly towards it. For a change, luck was on Hogg's side. As he was about to climb over the fence next to the stop and conceal himself in some bushes, he saw a bus approaching. Stepping aboard, he paid the fare going back to New Romney and alighted outside the old Town Hall. It was a small town with a few shops along the High Street and Hogg walked back along the road. At the corner of an alleyway he saw a sign pointing down an alley to The Coach House Coffee Shop. That would do him, he thought. Entering the cafe, he ordered coffee and a toasted cheese and ham sandwich. He knew he had lost them; for now.

It was now just before five thirty and the coffee shop closed at six. Hogg was in a bit of a quandary as to what he could do next. He now knew that cameras were watching for him everywhere and there were few people he could trust. Leaving his haven, he crossed the small road at the back and entered the churchyard opposite. He made his way round to the back of the church and sat on a bench among the ancient gravestones to await nightfall. When it was sufficiently dark, he left his haven and sneaked along Church Approach. A car turned into the narrow road and Hogg dived rapidly into a parking spot behind a doctor's surgery. The vehicle went past, the driver showing no sign of having seen him. Waiting on the corner until there was no traffic in sight, he crossed the main road quickly and with his head down, just in case there were cameras around that he had not spotted. A little farther along he took a turning to his left, deciding that keeping to the back streets was his best bet and, with more than a little relief, he came acroos a small bed and breakfast hotel on his right opposite another turning. He paid cash up front for five nights, deciding to remain inside the hotel all the while he was there, allowing the trail to go completely cold before venturing into the outside world again. It would almost be like being banged up in prison once more but at least, unlike his last incarceration, he had the choice of when he could leave this time.

Paul Gosling's helicopter had returned to Lydd Airport to refuel and allow them time to formulate a new plan. When the miniature steam train had arrived at Jefferstone Lane Station, Gosling's team and five local police officers were waiting on both sides of the tracks when the train pulled in. They systematically searched all the carriages before allowing the driver to take the train on its way. It became obvious Seeing police officers searching the train, one public spirited citizen informed them that a man had jumped out of the

81

moving carriage before it reached the station. Back in the helicopter once more, they back-tracked along the railway, sweeping slowly along beside the main road in the hope of finding him but it was hopeless. They had lost him once again.

Gosling called the result in on his mobile. He knew the reaction he would get from his superior and so was not surprised to get the verbal assault down the line. Finally, Whitehead calmed down enough to give him fresh instructions. Stand by at Lydd for any information gleaned from local cameras!

* * * *

WESTMINSTER, LONDON

SEPTEMBER 30TH. 1997

In Downing Street, Westminster, the Prime Minister shuffled through some papers on his desk, re-arranging them in order of importance for his attention later on in the day. The knock on the door he had been expecting came but it still caused him to jump and his senior secretary entered.

"The gentleman you were waiting for has arrived, Prime Minister," she said with a sweet smile. He nodded and told her to show the man in. The new arrival entered the room and walked with a confident gait to the desk wearing a navy blue, single breasted suit and carrying a dark brown, leather attache case which he placed on the floor at his feet. The Premier, wearing his customary grey, three piece suit, a gold watch chain across the front of his waistcoat, stood and looked the man up and down carefully. He appeared to be in his early to mid forties with short fair hair, fashionably cut. The wide shoulders, big hands, broad chest straining against the buttons of his jacket, solid square jaw and six foot two inch height gave the impression of an immensely powerful body beneath the well-cut, tailored clothes.

"I won't shake your hand, if you don't mind," the P.M. said with a thin smile, the tips of his fingers touching as he rested his hands in front of him. He continued, looking down at the desk top, unable to look the other man in the eye. "I don't need to know your name either. Suffice to say that you have been recommended by your superiors as the ideal man for this particular job." He paused as if waiting for a response. There was none. The other man simply stood in front of the enormous, leather topped desk, his hands clasped at his front, looking down at the thinning hair on the Minister' head. The head of Her Majesty's Government slid a thin, beige folder across the desk so that it almost fell off the other side, as if touching it would confirm his guilt. "In there you will find all the

83

details of your assignment. That document, once read will be shredded right here and will not leave this room. Are we clear?"

"Of course, sir. I have been instructed on what is required." Without waiting to be invited, the newcomer pulled out the visitor's chair, sat down and opened the folder, resting it on his crossed legs, his case still at his feet. The Prime Minister paced the room slowly from one wall to the other and back several times in complete silence, his footsteps muffled by the thickness of the carpet's pile, twirling his hands and fingers behind his back, occasionally stealing a glance at this man who he secretly feared, sitting in front of his desk reading calmly as if he were perusing the daily newspaper. There was an air of menace about the man that he found quite disconcerting. After ten minutes and having read through the documents twice, the man put down the folder and sat quite still, a slight frown upon his face as if in deep thought. The P.M. was given the impression that he was required to re-take his own seat and did so looking back across the desk.

"You understand what has to be done?"

"Just to be absolutely clear on this delicate matter, sir. The person in question is Lord Andrew Woolacott?"

"That is correct," the Minister replied, gingerly taking back the now closed folder that sat between them and then lowering his eyes so that he need not look at the other person in the room. "There may also be another person to be dealt with at some stage in the not too distant future but not just yet."

"I shall take the necessary steps, Prime Minister," the stranger said with the merest hint of a smile. He stood abruptly, turned and left the room without another word, closing the door gently behind him. The holder of the most important post in the land sat dumbfounded, staring at the closed door. In the strange man's eyes he had seen the shadow of death. This was a ruthless killer, one who was employed by the security services of necessity. He left number ten Downing Street by the same route he had entered, a private entrance accessed via Horseguards Parade at the rear. A black Range Rover was waiting there for him, the driver sitting patiently behind the wheel. The engine was started without a word exchanged between the two men and the vehicle purred softly away, arriving in the underground car park at their headquarters on Albert

84

Embankment next to the River Thames some ten minutes later due to the high volume of traffic. The passenger got out of the car and walked the four paces to the lift that would take him directly to the tenth floor of Section Six of Military Intelligence, otherwise known as the S.I.S. Building, MI6. He stepped out and swiped his I.D. card through a scanner before the heavy, bullet-proof glass doors slid open to allow him entry. Along the corridor, he went through a door to his right which led to an ante-room. The smart, pleasantly attractive middle-aged secretary behind the desk looked up at him as he entered.

"I'll let him know you are here, sir," she said with a polite smile and depressed a button beside the telephone. The other door on the far side of the room emitted a buzzing sound and the man pushed it open, striding through. Behind a glass desk sat Gilbert Howard, a well built man in his fifties, going bald with what was left of his hair around the sides and back turning to silver. Gold-rimmed glasses sat upon a somewhat bulbous, reddish nose, hovering above a pencil thin moustache. He sat back in his chair, resting his clasped hands on his ample stomach and looked up at the man.

"Well, Jonathan? Were you accepted?"

"Yes, sir," came the reply. "The P.M. gave me all the details." He sat down on an upright chair in front of the desk and crossed his legs before continuing. "I can confirm that the person the Government want out of the way is Lord Andrew Woolacott, your opposite number in MI5." Howard suddenly lurched forward and stared in disbelief.

"Old Woolly? …. The target is Lord Woolacott? Are you certain of this?"

"Absolutely. I've seen the folder with all the details of him, his houses in Pimlico and in the country. Dates, times and places of future established meetings, everything that would be required except a detailed itinerary." Gilbert Howard exhaled slowly and let his eyes fall to the desk top between his hands.

"Right then," he said at length, having carefully considered what he had just been told. "I'll leave everything to you. Let you get on with it but just remember, you're on your own on this one, old son. It has nothing to do with this department in any way whatsoever, is that clear?" His subordinate nodded.

"Of course, sir. I understand completely." He stood and walked back out, through the secretary's office and down one flight of stairs to his own much smaller office. Unlike Howard's plush suite overlooking the Thames, the view from this room took in the ends of the platforms for Vauxhall Station. Now came the planning stage. He set about making his plans by scribbling a few notes on a pad, arrows connecting different venues and dates. He felt that there would not be much of a problem and sat back in his chair, closing his eyes to think.

Jonathan Aubrey Wycke was born in nineteen fifty two to quite well off parents in Weybridge, Surrey. His father was the manager of three branches of Barclays Bank in South West London. Wycke attended the local boy's grammar school and, as was expected of him, went on to Eton College. At the age of twenty one he was accepted into Sandhurst Military College, training to be an officer. He was then seconded to the elite S.A.S Regiment, the British Special Forces unit. He was number four of the team that stormed the Iranian Embassy, ending the siege in 1981. His abilities became noticed by intelligence services and at the age of thirty seven he was approached by MI6 with an offer to join one of their specialist teams. He accepted readily and was integrated into their 'Special Operations' section. This was the department that made people disappear permanently. He was responsible directly to Gilbert Howard, head of MI6 and nobody else. The current case of Lord Woolacott's extermination would be his seventh such assignment in the five years he had been with the department. This one was a little different, though. Orders from on high on a need-to-know basis.

After sitting with his eyes closed for almost twenty minutes, he had formulated what he deemed to be a fool-proof plan of action that would do the job and leave no-one the wiser. He was certain that one of the team in the covert section on the third floor would be able to supply him with the necessary equipment so he went downstairs. On entering the open planned office, he espied an acquaintance on the far side, his head buried in a large book. He approached unseen, causing the man in a white coat and protective goggles to jump slightly when he was spoken to.

"Hello, Toddy, old sport," Wycke said with his customary smile, slapping the other man on the back. His warm smile belied the

86

ruthlessness of his character. Jeremy Todd looked up with a start.

"Jesus!" he exclaimed, closing his eyes in some relief. "Don't creep up on me like that while I'm doing this sort of work, John."

"Why? What are you up to at the moment?"

"Working out how to get this miniature explosive device hidden within the binding of this bloody book." He turned his eyes back to the stainless steel table top he was working on and scratched the back of his neck then looked back up at Wycke. He knew the man must want something from him or he would not have taken the trouble to come down the stairs himself. Any contact between them was usually made by the secure internal phone system. Wycke told him what was required.

"I need a syringe with the finest of needles, filled with some sort of jollop that will kill a man but make it seem like he's had a massive heart attack. What do you think? Can you do it?"

"Yes, of course. We already have something like that in store in the basement. It's called aconite or, to give it its full name, aconitum napellus, otherwise known as monkshood. An herbaceous perennial plant with beautiful blue or dark purple flowers. Found all over Western Europe, the Balkans and even in North America. Highly toxic, extremely poisonous if ingested or, in your case, injected. It was used on spears and arrows in ancient times."

"How does it work, Toddy?"

"Given in a high and concentrated dose by injection, it will bring about nausea, vomiting, paralysis and then death from heart failure within about three to five minutes from introducing the poison into the blood system." Wycke nodded his approval. It sounded ideal for his plan. "I can have enough to bring on heart failure put in to a syringe with a very fine needle. How does that sound for you?"

"Good man," he said. "Can you see to that for me, old boy? Quick as you like. Time and tide and all that, you know." He walked off with a spring in his step, whistling 'Moon River' softly to himself. Deciding that he would have to get the approval from Howard on his plan, he took the lift back up to the top floor. Howard's secretary smiled warmly at him as he exited the lift. When he was ushered into the inner sanctum, he outlined his plan to his chief.

"Only problem I can foresee, sir, is that the poison might be picked up on any post-mortem investigation. I am assured by the chaps downstairs that it is unlikely to be picked up, but it would be better to be prepared, just in case." Howard nodded wisely and thought for a moment.

"I think you can leave that to me, Jonathan," he stated firmly. "I can ensure that the right pathologist gets the job to record the death as being from heart failure. We have one that we use on a regular basis. Woollacott has already had one minor heart attack two or three years ago and it won't be completely out of the blue, especially given his appetite for food and drink and his heavy work-load. Just let me know when things get to that stage. I'll see if I can find out his itinerary and meetings for the foreseeable future." Howard turned his attention back to his laptop, indicating that the meeting had drawn to a conclusion. Wycke turned smartly and left the room, taking the stairs and heading for his own much smaller office.

The following morning, as he was about to leave his home at Hadley Green, in Barnet, Wycke's coded mobile phone buzzed. It was Howard, summoning him to the office immediately. A fifty minute ride on the tube, then a taxi journey brought him to the imposing S.I.S Building on the Embankment. Entering Howard's office, he was invited to sit by a hand gesture from the man.

"I have everything there is to know about Lord Woolacott here," he said, handing across a thick beige folder. "Your eyes only, Jonathan, obviously," he added with a knowing look. Wycke nodded.

"Of course, sir," he replied with the slightest trace of a smile. "If you don't mind, I'll read it here and then leave it with you. That way there is no chance of anyone else seeing it." Howard accepted the statement. The best way to deal with these matters was to keep everything close.

"I'll leave you to it then," he said as he stood and left the room. Wycke opened the folder and began to read. After ten minutes he had scanned the report but then went back to the beginning and read it through again, this time more carefully. It was three quarters of an hour later that Howard returned to the office, just as Wycke had finished perusing the documents.

"Well? Anything there that you can make use of?" he enquired nonchalantly, almost as if he were asking the time of a train.

"I'm certain that I can utilise this information, sir," Wycke responded as he pushed the folder back across the desk.

"Fair enough. It's in your hands and I don't want to know anything about it. Are we clear on that?"

"Absolutely. I just need clearance for a weapon and sufficient ammunition, sir. Just in case what I have in mind falls through and things get a bit sticky." Howard made an internal phone call to the armoury, giving his authorisation for the issue. Wycke's weapon of choice was always a Walther PPK automatic pistol with a Carswell silencer. Nothing more was said between the two men as Wycke stood and left the room. Howard sat back in his comfortable chair and thought that he was glad not to be in the well-heeled shoes of Lord Andrew Woolacott, especially with a man like Jonathan Wycke coming for him. He decided to make further discreet enquiries to find out what Woolacott had been involved in just recently. It didn't take him long, from reading internal reports and information gleaned from hearsay and office gossip to find out about Operation New Broom and the ramifications of the incident. He also gained a lot of knowledge of James Hogg and all his dealings.

Two days later on a Friday evening, Lord and Lady Woolacott arrived at the Grosvenor Hotel on Park Lane in the Mayfair district of Central London, attending a gala dinner to celebrate the retirement of Lord Marchand, a long term acquaintance and a fellow member of the House of Lords. Towards the end of the festivities, Woolacott left his table to go to the gentlemen's lavatory. As he stood at the urinal, he barely took any notice of the moustached waiter who entered and went into a cubicle behind him. Looking up towards the ceiling in relief as he started to urinate, he felt a sharp stabbing pain in the right side of his neck, almost like an insect sting and turned to see the waiter standing at his shoulder, a syringe in his hand, his face expressionless. Woolacott immediately began to feel weak at the knees, bile rising into his throat. As he started to fall forward towards the wall, he felt himself being dragged backwards into one of the cubicles and pushed down on to the toilet bowl. Trying unsuccessfully to regain his feet, he spontaneously vomited, covering his dress shirt front and trousers. He could not comprehend why the waiter was standing in front of him, his back to the closed door, just watching him. Suddenly, His Lordship's back stiffened and arched violently and an almost silent gasp left his lips. His eyes squeezed

89

shut in excruciating pain as the spasm released its grip on his body and Lord Woolacott breathed his last.

The entire episode had lasted a little less than three minutes. The waiter, having listened for movement outside and ensured there was none, left the cloakroom and made his way back down to the busy and bustling kitchens in the basement of the hotel, moving swiftly between the chefs and other staff and leaving unnoticed by the back door. Taking off his white jacket and rolling it into a tight ball, he walked quickly all the way through to Grosvenor Square where he entered a small mews off one corner of the quiet square. Once inside the mews and hidden from any prying eyes, he peeled off the fake black moustache, took off the heavy black-rimmed glasses and dark wig, stuffing everything in to the small hold-all he had secreted there behind the rubbish bins earlier that evening. Slipping into his sports jacket taken from the bag, he made his way to Oxford Circus Underground Station to begin his journey back home. Just before going down the escalator, he switched on his mobile phone and sent Gilbert Howard a text message of just one word; 'Blondin'. It was the codeword they had agreed upon for when the clandestine operation had been successfully completed.

Three quarters of an hour later, a nonchalant Jonathan Wycke left the tube at High Barnet station, the terminus for the line and took a taxi from the rank outside to his home, less than a mile away. He usually walked to his house from the station but this evening he felt he needed to unwind and relax a little.

A small, six inch column on page eleven of the following day's Daily Mail mentioned that Lord Andrew Woolacott, MBE, a senior official in the British security service, had died as a result of a suspected heart attack the night before whilst attending a gala evening for one of his colleagues. The article went on to give details of the grieving family and how much he would be missed.

Roger Whitehead, seated in his own fifth floor office, read the newspaper article with a great deal of suspicion although he accepted that his senior officer, being so overweight and unhealthy was most certainly in the high risk category for heart problems. It just appeared strange that his demise should occur at this fortuitous time. However, on the plus side as far as Whitehead was concerned, this would probably mean that he would be promoted to Head of Section

Five, a position he had coveted for many, many years, ever since being made up to Deputy Head of the department. He permitted a slight smile to creep across his face.

With no further recent sightings of Hogg, Whitehead was beginning to suspect that the wily man had somehow made his way out of the country by clandestine means, despite all sea ports and airports being on high alert for him. Even the small, provincial private airfields had received a circular for them to be on the look-out as well. Interpol and all the other foreign agencies were alerted to keep watch for any unusual activity that may lead to the wanted man being apprehended.

* * * *

NEW ROMNEY, KENT

OCTOBER 3RD. 1997

Jimmy Hogg left the safety of the Broadacre Hotel at eleven in the morning on the sixth day, fairly confident that the search for him had by now more than likely moved away from his current position in New Romney. His appearance had changed considerably since arriving. Now sporting a stubbly beard, he had also brushed his hair into a different style. He still had sufficient cash in his pocket, despite having to pay out for the bed and breakfast as well as takeaway meals he had been taking delivery of in the evenings. There was a charity shop almost at the corner and Hogg went in, purchasing a second hand flat cap and a maroon puffer jacket that altered the shape of his body too. Having obtained the telephone number of a local taxi company from the helpful, elderly lady who worked behind the counter in the shop, he called and arranged to be collected from the corner of the road, twenty yards away.

The taxi duly arrived and he asked to be taken to Ashford where he was set down at the top of the slope that led down to the station. As they had approached the station, he had spotted what he was seeking. A multi-storey car park. He walked back round to it and noted the cameras mounted on the walls at the entrance and the exit barriers. With his head bowed and the cap pulled well down over his eyes, he walked inside and went up the concrete staircase to the third floor. A pale blue Ford Granada near one of the corners was his target. Hogg selected a key from the large bunch in his pocket and tried the lock. On the fourth attempt it unlocked. The key slid easily into the worn ignition and the engine fired on the first try. Hogg cruised the car slowly down to the ground floor and stopped on one side, twenty yards short of the barrier. With no pre-paid ticket to get out of the car park, he needed to await the exit of another vehicle in order to follow it through the barrier. Only ten minutes later, his wish was granted as a car came down the ramp from an upper floor and stopped at the barrier. The driver inserted his card into the slot. The small green light came on and the barrier opened upwards, the car going through. Hogg had pulled the Ford right on to the other car's rear bumper and, as it moved forward, he went with it. The barrier had started to come down and just barely clipped the boot of the stolen Ford with a slight thud. He was out and had wheels that no-one knew about and headed straight for the M.20 motorway for London. He could lose himself there in the crowds and there were a few people he could trust who might be able to help him. Checking the fuel gauge, he was highly delighted to see that it was three quarters full, more than enough to get him to the capital. Once on the motorway, he kept to a steady seventy miles an hour, entering Central London without any problems an hour and a half later. He drove down the ramp and in to the underground car park beneath the Hilton Hotel in Park Lane. Parking in a bay on the second level down, he managed to lock the car and went up the concrete staircase to the roadway. He hoped it would be some time before the stolen car was found. With a little luck, they would not attribute the theft to him. His watch showed just after four in the afternoon and he was starving.

Keeping to the back streets and his head bowed, Hogg made his way through Shepherd's Market, crossing Regent Street and in to the district of Soho where he felt more at ease and knew his way around. He remembered a small cafe in Old Compton Street where he could get something to eat without anyone taking any notice of him. A large helping of steak and kidney pie with mashed potato and peas, swimming in thick gravy was more than enough to fill him. Two mugs of coffee later, it was just after six o'clock and beginning to get dark. It was time to make a move. The street outside the cafe was busy with people making their way home from work, too early for the more villainous inhabitants of Soho to be out and about. He walked slowly down Great Windmill Street and waited on the corner of Archer Street from where he had a good view of the doorway to Silk's Club. With scaffolding going up from the pavement where he stood for workmen to carry out repairs to the building he was beside, Hogg felt he would be safe and unseen from any prying eyes by stepping back into the doorway. It was over an hour and a half later that a huge, bearded man approached Silk's, walking with a rolling gait and jangling a bunch of keys. He unlocked and slid open the metal shutters that covered the front of the glass, opened the door and, securing it wide open with the clasp on the inside wall, went inside. Hogg knew the man as Rocky, the barman for the club. Another ten minutes passed before he saw Alan Randall come out of Ham Yard, almost beside the club. He had obviously parked his car there as was his habit. Randall disappeared inside the club and reappeared in the doorway a short while later, minus the black overcoat he had been wearing when he went in and nursing a white mug of coffee. Hogg watched him standing there for ten minutes or so and cautiously scanned the road in both directions while he patiently waited. He let an empty taxi pass and turn the far corner before stepping out from his concealment and crossing the street.

"Let us in, Al, for Christ's sake," he whispered urgently as he approached the door to the club. Randall immediately recognised his old friend and stood to one side, his eyes swiftly seeking any form of unexpected danger from the road as he sipped nonchalantly from his steaming coffee cup. Hogg went straight through the beaded curtain and into the small bar area, followed immediately by Randall.

"Fucking *hell*, Jimmy!" he exclaimed, pushing Hogg further into the club. "The Filth are looking for you everywhere, uniform *and* plain clothes. Word on the street is you've topped some reporter or something."

"It ain't true, Al. My life it ain't," Hogg retorted with a trace of a sob cracking his voice. "It's to do with what I told you in Bar Italia. They're trying to fit me up just so that I get pulled in. If they get me, no-one'll ever hear from me again. I'll be dead." He slumped against the end of the bar, his head in his hands. This was all getting too much for him now. Hogg was small time and couldn't cope with this amount of pressure. Randall took him by the arm and led him to a fire exit at the rear of the building. Opening it up, he led the burglar out into Ham Yard. Using a remote controlled key fob, he unlocked his car with a press of the button and nodded towards it.

"Go and sit in there, Jim," he instructed with an air of authority. "Get in the back and lie down on the floor. See if you can grab a few hours sleep. You look terrible. I'll see if I can bring you out something to eat later. I finish work just after three o'clock and I'll take you back to my place. You'll be safe enough there until we can work out a plan." He watched as Hogg shuffled across the yard and opened the back door. Sliding inside, he disappeared from view. Randall depressed the button once more to lock the car. The fugitive made himself as comfortable as he could, stretched across the whole width of the car. He dozed intermittently but real sleep eluded him. He had just nodded off for the fourth time when the car was unlocked at three fifteen as Randall finished working. The doorman got behind the wheel and started the engine.

"Stay down and out of sight, Jim," he instructed without turning his head as he drove the car out of Ham Yard and turned left into Great Windmill Street. It was not until they were passing through Finsbury Park fifteen minutes later that Randall told Hogg it was now safe for him to sit up. "You can doss down at my flat for a couple of nights, but only until we can sort something out for you. Okay?" Hogg said that it was and profusely thanked his old school friend. Randall had a one bedroomed flat in Edmonton, almost above a florists in Church Street and accessed from a side road where he parked out of sight of any nosey neighbours. They both went quickly up the stone staircase behind the shops, along the outside landing and inside the flat. Randall switched the electric kettle on and spooned coffee into two mugs. "I've got the beginnings of an idea to get you out of the way, Jim, but I'll have to make a few phone calls to see how the land lies first."

"Fine by me," Hogg replied with a heavy sigh. "I've just about had enough of this lark, Al. They're out to kill me and I ain't even got anything to protect myself with. Haven't got a gun, have you, Alan?" he asked hopefully. Randall appeared to think about this for a moment before replying.

"Not right at this minute, mate, but I may be able to sort something out for you." He disappeared into another room, taking his mobile phone from his pocket as he went. Hogg gratefully sipped at his coffee. It was now gone four in the morning and he had been awake for twenty two hours, the tiredness beginning to get to him now. His head drooped and his chin rested upon his chest as he sat at the kitchen table. He was shaken back to life by Randall's hand on his shoulder. Glancing up at the clock on the wall, he was astounded to find that almost four hours had passed. The clock showed ten minutes to eight.

"I can get hold of a gun for you, Jim. It'll mean pulling in a few favours and I can't pick it up from my contact in Leytonstone until later this afternoon," Randall said with a reassuring smile. "Go and crash out on my bed, mate," he continued, taking the now cold coffee mug away and placing it in the sink. Hogg got slowly to his feet and mumbled his thanks as he dragged himself into the bedroom, falling face down on the double bed fully clothed. He was instantly asleep.

Later that afternoon, Randall woke his slumbering guest and told him that he was off to meet his contact, hoping to return in about two hours. Hogg was told to make himself at home and help himself to food. The front door closed and he heard Randall lock it behind him as he left.

Having helped himself to some cheese and bread, Hogg settled down to wait at the kitchen table once again. That was when doubts began to enter and infect his already confused mind. What if Randall was going to sell him out to the police? Maybe he had been offered money to turn the fugitive in to the authorities. After all, he didn't owe Hogg anything, did he? They were only old school pals after all. By the time he had finished eating, he had convinced himself that the police were already on their way to the flat, probably already had it surrounded by armed officers. He went to the window that looked out on to the main road, peering round the edge of the curtain. Nothing appeared to be out of the ordinary but then it wouldn't, would it? The Old Bill would be more than a little discreet, especially as they would more likely than not want to snatch him without too many members of the public noticing. That way he could be spirited away and taken out of existence with no-one the wiser. He thought about making a run for it, maybe get to his sister's house only a quarter of a mile away; but then he realised that they would have that under observation too. That was how they had almost caught him before. He made his mind up. He would run the hundred yards to Lower Edmonton Station and jump on the first train that came in, wherever it was going. Worry about where he was later. As he reached the front door of the flat, it opened and Randall stepped in. Hogg frantically tried to look over his shoulder to see if anyone was with him. Randall put a hand on his upper arm and frowned.

"Steady on, Jimmy," he said, still frowning. "What's got into you?

You're shaking like a leaf.'"

"I dunno, Al. I thought that maybe you had grassed me up or something. I don't really know what the fuck I'm doing." It was then that he noticed the carrier bag that Randall was holding. His host steered him back in to the kitchen and placed the bag on the table, motioning Hogg to sit down.

"In there is what you were asking for," he said, nodding at the bag. "I've gone to a lot of trouble to get hold of that for you." Hogg gazed at the bag, fear etched upon his face which had aged considerably.

"What is it?" he asked, with more than a little trepidation.

"It's a Smith and Wesson Model 64, six shot revolver with a stainless steel four inch barrel, a bit short and stubby so you'll be able to keep it well hidden. There are four quick-loading cartridges filled with bullets in the bag as well. All you have to do is flick open the drum, shake out the empties then push the new cartridge pack in to reload with six fresh bullets." Randall proceeded to show how it was done and made it look so easy. "It's as simple and quick as that." Hogg expressed his concern and said that he was worried about using a weapon. "Let's face it, Jimmy," Randall told him in response with a sigh. "You've got some pretty nasty people who are hell bent on getting to you that I wouldn't fancy going up against myself, so you are definitely going to need this gun at some stage, I reckon, my old mate." Hogg took the gun and weighed it in his hand. It somehow gave him a feeling of strength, power even, thinking that maybe he *could* deal with the problem with this weapon at his disposal.

Two days later, Randall handed him a driving licence photocard and the keys to an old, dark blue Peugeot 405 estate car that was parked in Lyon Road, next to the entrance to the flat. He had acquired it from an 'acquaintance' who had owed him a favour from way back and this was his way of paying it off. The vehicle had seen better days but Randall assured Hogg that it was roadworthy with a reasonably good engine. It had a valid M.O.T. certificate, was taxed and insured for Peter Kettlety and that was the name that accompanied Hogg's photograph on the forged licence card. He also handed over a cheap, disposable mobile phone.

"There's twenty quid pre-paid credit on that just in case you need to get in touch in an emergency. I've entered my number into it for you. *Don't* go calling anyone else on it, understand?" he warned.

Hogg assured him that he wouldn't. "How are you off for money, Jim?" Randall asked his old friend as he prepared to leave the flat.

"I've got a few quid, Al. Thanks anyway," Hogg replied with a smile. He was grateful for all the help his old partner had given him. Now dressed in a completely different set of clothes donated by Randall, his hair now longer, dyed black and sporting a good sized beard and moustache which completed the transformation, Hogg hefted the holdall he had been given with spare clothing inside. He slung it over his shoulder and shook Randall by the hand. "Thanks, mate," he said and meant it. "You've helped me no end and I won't forget it."

"Just make sure you stay out of the limelight and tucked away where they won't find you." Hogg promised that he would and left the flat, throwing his bag on to the back seat of the car. It was ten thirty five in the morning. Randall had provided him with the address of a cottage on Bodmin Moor in Cornwall that belonged to his ageing aunt. She was now languishing in a nursing home in Okehampton and had adamantly refused to give up the cottage 'just in case' she was ever able to go back there. Stopping off for supplies as he passed through the town, Hogg continued on the A.30 dual carriageway and turned off to the right, as instructed towards St. Breward. He turned right again at a T-junction after two miles and found the cottage a few hundred yards farther along the road on the right hand side. It was now just before five thirty in the evening. Using the key that Randall had provided him with, he let himself in. The creaking front door opened directly into the living room. The place had an eerie, musty odour to it and, to enhance the feeling of antiquity, he noted that all the furniture was from an age prior to his. The sort that his old grandfather had furnished his house in Enfield with. A chintz two seater sofa and armchair to match. No sign of a television. A walnut dresser and cabinet stood against one wall, filled to overflowing point with plates and knick-knacks, dust gatherers. He ran his index finger along the edge of the dresser and it came away with a thick coating of grey dust. Going through to the kitchen did nothing to lift his spirits either. An ancient, blue enamel gas stove on legs was against the farthest wall and had obviously seen better days. The kettle that sat upon one of the rings was beginning to rust. It was one of the old whistling types. Hogg took

98

it across to the once white Butler sink under the window and emptied the dregs of water that had been left inside it. A couple of house spiders that had made the spout their home scuttled their way across the bottom of the sink in fear. He turned on the tap to flush them, scrabbling, down the plug-hole. At first, the water began to build up in the sink until the pressure eventually sent it down the hole with a gush. There had probably been something in the waste pipe. He rinsed the kettle and emptied it, half filled it with water and set it back on the stove. He went to the cupboard as Randall had instructed and turned on the main gas supply handle and turning the electricity switch on before returning to the appliance, rotating the knob and hearing the hiss of escaping gas. He lit the ring beneath the kettle and started to unpack his shopping. Having done that, he found some china teacups in a cabinet, washed one under the running cold tap and put instant coffee granules in it with a spoonful of sugar. He leaned with the knuckles of both hands on the table and, to his amazement, almost immediately heard the shrill whistle from the kettle as it started to boil. He hadn't thought it would heat up so quickly. Pouring the boiling water into the cup, he added milk and stirred before taking the cup back into the living room. He noticed the steep, wooden staircase that led upstairs and headed up, the cup in one hand and the other on the bannister rail. At the top, there were three doors. Inside the first he found the toilet and a small bath and washbasin. Dust had settled everywhere. The second door he went through was a bedroom with an old bed, covered with a now dusty candlewick bedspread. After surveying the room for a few moments, he opened the third door to find that it was being used as a storage or junk room. Broken and worn out pieces of furniture, and other pieces of trash were strewn everywhere. A small mouse darted out from the pile and went past his foot at an astounding speed. It caused Hogg to jump, spilling some of the hot coffee on to his hand. He swore out loud and then smiled to himself at his outburst. Going back downstairs, he drained his cup and left it on the draining board before taking his bag back up to the bedroom. He felt exhausted from the long drive and pulled off the bedspread to find a bare mattress beneath it. He laid himself back on top of it and was asleep within seconds.

When Hogg awoke, daylight was streaming through the thin,

flowered curtains from strong sunlight. It took him a moment or two to remember where he was, then put his shoe-less feet to the floor and, with some effort, stood up and stretched. He went through to the bathroom and splashed cold water over his face and neck. He had forgotten to switch the water heater on. In the kitchen downstairs, he made coffee and toast from under the oven grill. Fifteen minutes later he was refreshed and ready to fully explore his new, temporary home. He familiarised himself with the cottage, its light switches, boiler system and heating. The weather had not been too kind recently and there was the threat of colder to come.

It took him several hours to clean the place up to a reasonable condition and he was surprised to find it was now a quarter to four in the afternoon. Wiping dust and sweat from his forehead, Hogg took the five large, black plastic sacks out the front door and down the garden path, leaving them just inside the gate. As he turned to go back, a police car came cruising round the bend in the road. He noticed that the only occupant was the driver. Hogg thought about running for the cottage to get the gun but had second thoughts. He reasoned that if they were coming for him they would not have sent just a single copper, so he stood still and watched the vehicle approach. The woodentop behind the wheel was looking intently at him as the car came to a halt beside the gate. The uniform got out in a casual manner, putting on his cap.

"Afternoon," he said as he came round the front of the car, pushing his cap on to the back of his head. "This is old Mrs. Trevelyan's place. And who might you be?" The man stood beside his car with his hands on his hips, his brows knitted tightly together in a questioning manner.

"I'm Peter Kettlety," Hogg replied with a smile and held out his hand in greeting. "Mrs. Trevelyan's nephew, Alan, has asked me to come down and look after the place while she is in the nursing home. He's asked me to clean it up as it had got into a bit of a mess." The officer appeared to be happy with the reply. He shook Hogg by the hand and nodded, returning the smile.

"Oh, I see," he responded. "Yes, I know Alan. Used to come down here a lot when he was younger. The old girl has a bit of a soft spot for him." He gazed down at the pile of rubbish bags and shook his head. "They won't get collected for just over a week," he said.

"Bin collection only takes place once a month out here in the sticks." He ended the sentence with a series of 'tuts' as if disgusted by the state of affairs that the local council had left them all in. "Well, I'll leave you to it then, Peter," the policeman said and turned back to his vehicle. The engine started and he pulled away with a wave of his hand. Hogg simply nodded and couldn't believe his luck. Here they were, Old Bill looking everywhere for him and he had just passed the time of day with one. He turned and ambled contentedly back to the cottage door, trying his best to control the shaking in his arems and the jelly-like feeling that was creeping down his thighs. As soon as the policeman had gone, Hogg called Randall on his burner phone and told him what had happened. Randall said that he should not worry and that he knew the copper and would sort it all out so that he stayed away from the cottage.

Police Sergeant Tony Boyens parked his patrol car outside the two bedroomed police house he shared with Cora, his wife of thirty one years. Although based in the small village of St. Breward, his patch covered the villages of Lank, Churchtown and Michaelstow as well, some twenty square miles. He had been a police officer for thirty six years and was just waiting for his up-coming sixtieth birthday before retiring. The Devon & Cornwall Constabulary had decided to close his out of the way police office but his long-standing friend, the Chief Constable, had promised to keep it going until that date. Arrangements had been put into place for him to take over the property when it was no longer needed and that suited Boyens just fine. He felt too old to be messing around moving house. He had spent quite a bit of his own money keeping the place looking nice and besides, it was right opposite the village pub. He only needed to stagger across the road at closing time.

At five feet eight inches tall, Tony Boyens had only just met the minimum height requirement for joining the force. As the years progressed, so did his girth, putting on considerable weight. He had now accepted the fact that his waistline would never decrease, he enjoyed Cora's cooking too much for that. Also, whenever out in his patrol car, he was always being offered tea and biscuits or cake and he felt it impolite to refuse such kind offers. He felt that he was like a parish priest and that the people he met on his rounds were his parishioners.

Walking in the front door beneath the blue lamp over the porch, he had a frown on his face as he took off his utility belt with radio, handcuffs and all the other equipment that police officers were now laden down with. At least out here in the countryside he did not feel the need to wear the cumbersome, protective anti-stab vest that others had to wear in the bigger towns. The worst that happened here was a sheep being hit by a car, and that only became a serious matter if the driver was under the influence of alcohol.

"What's that look for, luvvy?" Cora asked as she poured his tea from the pot.

"Not sure just yet, my darlin'," Boyens replied, still frowning. He placed his cap on the table and rubbed his chin "I passed by old Gladys Trevelyan's place just now and there's a young fella there, down from London. Says he's cleaning the house up for his friend, young Alan, her nephew. You remember him, don't you?" She stopped and gazed up at the ceiling for a moment, as if the answer was written there. After a few seconds she smiled and nodded vigorously.

"Oooh yes," she said at last. "I remember him now. Nice lad, always wore a suit when he was here."

"There's something not quite right there, I feel," the sergeant continued. "I think I'll pop into Oakie tomorrow and have a word with Gladys at the nursing home, just to make sure everything's tickety-boo."

"Well, if you're going into Okehampton you can pick up that dry cleaning for me," she said.

When he arrived at the nursing home the following day, he found Gladys Trevelyan watching the huge television from a wing-backed armchair in the resident's lounge. She beamed when she saw him enter the room. She had known him since his first day in the village.

"Anthony, dear," she said warmly. "What a lovely surprise. What brings you here?" She had always used his full name and he hated it with a passion but had never corrected her. With a sigh, he slowly lowered himself down into the comfortable, armchair next to hers.

"How are you, Glad?" he asked with genuine affection. He could always rely on the old girl for a cup of tea and a couple of chocolate digestive biscuits when out on patrol and passing her cottage.

"Oh, I'm fine, my love. They look after us very well here, you know. Nothing's too much trouble for them. I've got my little room, my own telly and I know there's always someone on hand just in case. I like to come down here though where there is always someone to talk to." She looked at him sideways before continuing. "I'm not silly, Tony. I know that I can't keep that cottage going by myself any more" Boyens smiled at the elderly lady. From what he could see, most of the other residents were nodding off or in a state of total slumber despite the noise from the over loud television. She was probably grateful to have somebody sensible to chat with.

"I passed by your place yesterday and found some chap there. Friend of yours?" he asked in a friendly manner, leaning forward to help himself to a custard cream biscuit from the plate on the table.

"Oh, that will be Peter," she replied, her false teeth flashing a warm smile at the man. "He's a friend of Alan's. You must remember young Alan, my nephew?" Boyens said that he did. "Well, Alan has asked him to do a bit of tidying up for me. Apparently, Peter and his wife have separated and he has nowhere to live just now so this suits us both, do you see, Anthony?" Boyens nodded and continued to chat with her for another half hour before leaving, satisfied that there was nothing to concern him. All worries had subsided by now. Gladys may be getting on a bit, well in to her eighties but she still had all her marbles. She stood at the window and saw the policeman drive out of the private car park. She continued to watch until the police car turned the corner at the top of the hill then took her mobile phone from her handbag. She punched a preset number and listened to the comforting purr of the ring tone.

"Sergeant Boyens has just this minute left here in his car," she said when the call was answered.

"Thanks, Auntie Glad," Alan Randall said, smiling to himself.

* * * *

BODMIN MOOR, CORNWALL

OCTOBER 12TH. 1997

Having received no further unwanted attention since speaking to Alan Randall five days earlier, Hogg felt it was at last safe to go in to the village for fresh groceries as his supplies were dwindling severely. He still had quite a bit of his cash left but that too was depleted to a great extent. He arrived at the village general store which also served as the Post Office just after eight o'clock that morning. Loading up his holdall with provisions, as an afterthought he picked up a copy of the Daily Mail newspaper from the rack just inside the door and tucked it under his arm. He now had a one mile hike back to the cottage. Setting off at a brisk pace, he had almost reached the end of the row of houses on the outskirts of the small village when he heard the noise of a car engine approaching from behind. From the sound, he could tell it was slowing down. He turned to his right as Sergeant Boyens pulled up beside him in his patrol car. The passenger window went down electronically.

"You look as if you could do with a lift, Peter," he said with a wide grin and indicating the heavy bag slung over one shoulder. Hogg thought that it would look suspicious to refuse and, reluctantly, accepted the offer, sitting with the bag on his lap and the newspaper resting on top of it. Only two minutes later he said farewell to the officer outside the cottage and lugged the bag up to the front door. Things seemed to be going quite well for him. It wasn't the first time that Jimmy Hogg had been wrong.

Whilst sitting in the passenger seat, the front page of his folded newspaper had a small column on the right hand side about the wanted murderer and spy. Tony Boyens' keen eye had spotted it and it had registered on his brain. He carefully studied the side profile of his passenger as he drove. Upon returning to his office, he took out all the information that had come through to him about the wanted man. He had simply filed it all in a drawer when it had arrived. This wasn't the sort of place a fugitive would come to. The more he pored over the photographs, the more certain he was but doubt still lingered. The man's profile view was exactly right as was his height and age. Boyens didn't want to call in the heavy mob all the way from Newquay which was where the nearest armed response unit was permanently stationed unless he was absolutely certain. He telephoned his Chief Inspector in Bodmin and told him of his concerns.

Chief Inspector Malcolm Flack was a muscular man with a shock of silvery-grey hair and military moustache. He had been in the force for almost twenty years and knew Boyens personally. He didn't think the man would jump to such conclusions unless he had good cause. After listening to what he had to say, Flack thought for a few moments then made a decision.

"You say he was in the front seat of your car this morning, Tony?" Flack asked.

"That's right, sir. Sitting right next to me and I got a good look at his profile from the side."

"Right. Here's what to do. Download the footage from your car's interior camera and send it over to me personally. I'll get someone up here to have a good look at it too and we'll take it from there." Boyens said that he would get on to it immediately. He hadn't been this excited since his wedding night.

Less than fifteen minutes after sending the footage to Flack, the landline telephone at his elbow rang.

"Tony, you lovely lad," Flack almost shouted down the line. "The experts have looked at it and they think it's *definitely* him. There's an armed response unit already on its way to you from Newquay as we speak and there is also a team of spooks coming down from London by helicopter. It's a toss up as to who gets to you first. What they want you to do is to keep your car out of sight but keep an eye on the cottage to make sure that he goes nowhere." Sergeant Tony Boyens was sweating as he listened to the instructions. "Under no circumstances are you to approach the man, Tony. He's a killer and I don't want any heroics. Do you understand?" Boyens asserted that he did. There was no way he was going to get shot at with only a few mere months to go before retiring. He put down the phone and went out to his car. He decided that he would park a quarter of a mile before the bend and walk the rest of the way. Out of breath due to his lack of fitness, he was breathing heavily when he came to the bend a few hundred yards before the cottage, secreting himself behind one of the enormous evergreen, spiky gorse bushes covered with their tiny yellow flowers.

By the merest of chance, at the same time that Boyens had answered the call from Chief Inspector Flack, Jimmy Hogg had walked out of the back door of the cottage with the intention of hiking four miles overland, following the De Lank River to the towering hill called Brown Willy that stood a little over four hundred feet high to the north-east. His intention was to climb it and see the view from the top. Boredom was getting to him a little, especially with no television in the cottage. He had Randall's revolver tucked into his belt at the back with the intention of trying his luck at rabbit shooting. After twenty minutes of hard going, he heard the sound of a helicopter, ten seconds before it came into view over the hill. Hogg threw himself flat amongst the tall grass and reeds beside the river bank. The appearance of a low-flying helicopter was not a good sign. Out there in the open space of the moor, he then heard the shrill scream of police sirens many miles distant but gradually increasing in volume as they headed his way. Looking back over his shoulder, he saw the helicopter begin its descent into fields on the outskirts of St. Breward. He now knew it was Government men coming for him. Leaping to his feet, he started to run. Deciding that his best bet was to get to some form of civilisation and hijack a car, he headed off to his right towards where he knew the main dual carriageway was. A little over ten minutes later he was running across the main trunk road and into the village of Bolventor. A blue Mini Cooper was just pulling in to the car park of the Jamaica Inn Restaurant. A young woman was behind the wheel. Hogg opened the driver's door and thrust the gun into the petrified girl's face.

"Keep quiet and move across to the passenger seat," he ordered. The woman opened her mouth as if about to scream. "Don't you dare, if you want to live," Hogg hissed at her through clenched teeth. It had the desired effect. Her mouth clamped tightly shut. Although with tears streaming down her cheeks causing mascara to run like tramlines, she obeyed with some difficulty because of the cramped space in the car and the gear-stick between the front seats. The engine was still running as Hogg slid behind the wheel, still pointing the gun at the girl. "Now you're not going to be hurt or attacked or anything like that as long as you sit quietly and do nothing. Do you understand what I'm saying?" She nodded mutely, choking back sobs. Hogg noted that the fuel tank was almost full. Exactly what he wanted. With the gun nestling in his lap, he engaged first gear and set off, crossing the A.30, sweeping round a long bend and then joining the main road towards what he considered to be the safety of London.

As Hogg had been running across the moor, Gosling and his team of armed men burst in through the front door of Gladys Trevelyan's little cottage, their guns stretched out in front of them in both hands. Two of them rushed headlong up the stairs while the other two scoured the ground floor rooms and garden. The property was surrounded by heavily armed police officers wearing masks and helmets. It didn't take them long to realise that the place was empty.

"I thought you said he was in here," Gosling barked at Sergeant Boyens. The policeman wasn't going to take any shit from this London spook.

"Well he went *in* there and he hasn't come *out* since I've been keeping watch so he must have left before I got here, don't you think?" The look he gave Gosling said it all. This provincial copper was no pushover. Gosling turned his fury on to another officer standing by one of the police vans.

"You," he said, jabbing a finger towards the luckless officer. "Get your fucking dog out of the van and try to find him, for Christ's sake. Surely it can pick up a scent from the clothing he's left behind?"

"We'll give it a go, sir," he replied with a hint of a sneer. These bastard twats come down here from the big city and think we're bloody peasants, he thought. "If he's out there, my dog'll get him!" With the Alsatian dog on the end of a long stretch of rope, they all set off at a slow trot across the moor, the dog with its nose to the ground, following exactly in Hogg's footsteps.

By the time the poor, frazzled and worn out dog had led his handler and the other hunters to the edge of the main road near Bolventor, Hogg was sixty miles away, passing Taunton on the M.5 motorway. His intention was to join the M.4 which would take him

107

all the way to London. What he had not taken into account was the CCTV in the car park of the Jamaica Inn. One of the searching armed officers had gone in to the restaurant having spotted the cameras and asked to view any footage. They easily spotted the hijack and knew which car their quarry was in.

However, Hogg was not so complacent and had a nagging idea that they would be on his tail before long. Just after junction twenty two on the motorway, he pulled in to the service station and then headed for the exit again. He drove along the slip road that led back on to the motorway and then brought the car to a stop. He got out and ordered the young woman back into the driving seat.

"There you are, love," he said with a weak smile. "Sorry about that but I'm in a bit of a pickle, I'm afraid. It was my only chance." The girl looked at him with frightened eyes as she made her way back across to the drivers seat. "Now you just get going and don't stop until you get to the next junction, alright?" He stood back from the door and she crunched the car into gear and pulled away with the front wheels spinning, causing a passing vehicle to blast its horn and swerve out into the second lane. Hogg watched the car disappear in to the distance and then turned and jogged back to the edge of the service area. He ducked into the bushes and made his way round to the lorry park.

He now knew about cameras and was wise to them. Within five minutes he had found a lorry that had a London address on the door and with a load that he could easily secrete himself in. There was the chance that it may not be going to London but he was prepared to take that chance just to get away from his pursuers who he knew would not be too far behind, especially once the girl in the Mini had told them where he had left her. Not long after he had wedged himself within some machinery on the back of the truck, he heard the driver climb into the cab and the heavy diesel engine thundered into life. The large lorry gradually made its way past the fuel pumps, down the slip road and joined the motorway. It quickly picked up speed and roared along the tarmac at sixty miles an hour.

A little under thirty minutes later, Hogg was pleased to note that the vehicle had now joined the M.4 motorway. At least he knew he was going in the right direction. He used the burner phone from his pocket to call Randall to let him know to expect a visit. Randall

108

wasn't happy and told him so, hanging up the call. Hogg put the phone away in his pocket and made himself comfortable as best he could. It was at this point, lulled by the steady throb of the engine and the rocking movement of the vehicle that he nodded off into a semi sleep.

He awoke with a start as the lorry driver harshly applied the brakes. Hogg sneaked a look out and found they had left the motorway and were now on a busy high street somewhere, stopped at traffic lights. There were too many pedestrians and other cars around for him to climb out from his hiding place so he lay low, awaiting his chance. It came ten minutes later, when the truck pulled off the main road and into a side street, coming to a halt outside a factory of some sort. Before the driver had even left his cab, Hogg was out and walking quickly away. On reaching the major road, he turned right and spotted a black taxi coming towards him with its yellow 'For Hire' light on. He flagged it down and climbed in.

"Where to, Guv?" the driver enquired over his shoulder whilst surveying his passenger in his mirror.

"You're gonna think this is funny," Hogg began, "but I fell asleep on the bus and I've got no idea of where I am." He laughed a little and lowered his head to chuckle as if in embarrassment. The driver smiled and thought that his passenger was probably the worse for drink.

"You're just outside Richmond, mate, now where do you want to go?" The passenger appeared to be contemplating his options before replying while the taxi was still stationary, the engine idling.

"The nearest self-drive car hire firm, I think."

"You might just be lucky," the man told him. "I think they close at five thirty so you've only got about a quarter of an hour."

"Well let's crack on then, shall we?" The cabbie shrugged his shoulders and pulled the vehicle away from the kerb. Nothing more was said until they stopped ten minutes later beside a Hertz rental company. There was just over seven pounds on the meter so Hogg pushed a ten pound note through the opening in the glass partition that separated driver from passengers.

"Keep the change, pal," he said and climbed out with his head bowed, slamming the door behind him and watching the cab drive away in search of his next fare. Walking quickly up to the door of

109

the Hertz Rental company, he went in and up to the desk inside. A young woman looked up at him in surprise and automatically smiled a welcome, although her eyes said otherwise. The last thing she wanted right now was someone coming in to hire a car just five minutes before it was time to go home. The paperwork alone took fifteen minutes at the very least. She glanced up at the clock on the side wall. Five twenty five. Bastard!

"Hello," said Hogg warmly. "I need to hire a car as quickly as possible. I don't care what car it is or how much it costs," he continued, "and I shall probably need it for two or three days." Now that was something completely different, she thought. She could rent him the most expensive one that was available at the time and get a higher commission for her troubles. Fifteen minutes later he, as Peter Kettlety, was driving away in a brand new Ford Focus with just sixty odd miles on the clock.

Having driven the car away from the rental firm, he found a sign which indicated the motorway. Getting on to the M.25 orbital motorway, he just drove with no destination in mind at that time, just a desire to keep moving. It was soon after eight in the evening when he turned off on to the dual carriageway road that would lead him to Southend-On-Sea in Essex. He figured that, being a seaside town, there would be plenty of chances of securing somewhere to stay on a temporary basis. Either an out-of-season bed and breakfast guest house or perhaps a caravan would suffice for his needs. He drove into a multi-storey car park in the town centre and killed the engine on one of the middle floors. Letting the driver's seat back, he closed his weary eyes, relaxed and allowed himself to doze off into a fitful sleep.

* * * *

MI5 HEADQUARTERS

OCTOBER 13TH 1997

In his plush office on the sixth floor of Thames House on the North bank of the River Thames, Roger Whitehead settled his lean frame back into the soft, comfortable chair that had previously been occupied by Lord Andrew Woolacott, now deceased. Whitehead had been appointed as temporary head of MI5 until his promotion had been fully approved by the Prime Minister and his Cabinet. The vast office still smelled of the residue of His Lordship's enormous Havana cigars. With a contented sigh, he got up from the seat and wandered across, standing with his hands clasped behind his back at the huge floor to ceiling windows with small panes, looking out across Lambeth Bridge towards ancient Lambeth Palace, the London home of the Archbishop of Canterbury. Slightly to his left was the Southern end of Westminster Bridge and Waterloo Station. He could just see the enormous London Eye on the South Bank.

"Where the hell are you right now, Mister Hogg?" he asked himself out loud. The whereabouts of the former cat burglar were still a bit of a mystery and worried him immensely, causing him sleepless nights. Gosling had been sent down to Cornwall following a frantic telephone call from Devon & Cornwall police. They thought they had found Hogg holed up in a remote cottage on the moors and were sending an Armed Response Unit to the area. With luck, Gosling would get there first and deal with the problem once and for all. His biggest fear was that the man may manage to get abroad and have his story published in one of the foreign newspapers that MI5 would have no control over.

Looking to his right along Millbank, he could just make out the building complex of his opposite number in MI6 on the South side of the river by Vauxhall Bridge. Thankfully, they had no idea that it was his department that had come up with the idea of killing the second most powerful woman in the world; and now with Lord Woolacott out of the picture, Whitehead could take all the credit for himself. He intended to do just that when he met with the Prime Minister later in the day. Even his underling, Paul Gosling was unaware of the plot, probably the most audacious and heinous since the amateur attempts by Guido Fawkes to blow up the Houses of Parliament. Every person who knew of the assassination plot had been taken care of and the knowledge lay now with just himself, the P.M. and whichever person above him who gave the initial order. Whitehead had his suspicions but nothing else, nothing concrete. It would have to remain that way out of necessity. His coded mobile phone bleeped insistently, bringing him back to reality and the present. It was Paul Gosling, calling in. He snatched up the handset and answered, hoping that it would be good news.

"We appear to have temporarily lost him again, I'm afraid, sir," he heard the plaintive voice down the phone. "He seems to have more bastard lives than a cat! He hi-jacked a young girl's Mini and got out at the motorway service station slip-road. We've checked all the CCTV coverage and there's no trace of him anywhere. It's my bet that he's holed up somewhere quite close or maybe even tried to make his way in to Bristol. It's not that far away and he could be trying to lose himself in a big city." Whitehead sighed audibly and with a great deal of irritation in his voice.

"Alright, alright. Stay down there until we can get something definite on his whereabouts." Slamming the mobile phone down hard on the desk top, he sat back in the leather chair and tried to think. This was not going as planned. How could a second rate cat burglar get away for so long without breaking cover? His red desktop phone rang and he shook himself from his reverie to answer it.

"Roger, old boy," said a familiar voice. It was Gilbert Howard from MI6. The bastard. It was as if he had some sort of telepathic power. Whitehead gave a brief pause before answering him. The man never called unless there was something wrong or there was a flap on.

"Hello, Gil, and what can I do for you?"

"Might be more of a case of what *I* can do for *you*, my boy," came

112

the retort. "Come and have lunch with me in our restaurant. They do a half decent steak and kidney pie, you know. I'm sure it will be worth your time. Unless, of course, you have something else on at the moment?" The wily old dog was up to something, he knew. Either that or he was going to attempt to gain some kind of inside information from him over a meal on his home ground.

"Well I do have one or two things on at the moment, Gil but if you're willing to buy me a decent lunch, I shall present myself at your offices at one thirty sharp," Whitehead replied with a smile, slowly replacing the handset. The crafty old boy wasn't going to catch him out. He was alert and on his guard already. Fore-warned was fore-armed. He went back to the large windows and resumed his stare at the MI6 Building in the far distance. Now what the hell was Howard up to? he thought to himself. He had no answer at that point in time but was determined to find out before he left the plush in-house restaurant over the river.

At one twenty five, Whitehead produced his I.D. to the armed, uniformed security man at the door to MI6 and again at the information desk where a beefy man in a more than necessary bulging jacket made an internal telephone call in a whispered voice. Just over a minute later, the lift hissed to a stop and Jeanette Gaye, Howard's elegant secretary of many years standing, clip-clopped across the polished floor in her black, equally polished high-heeled shoes, wearing a lipstick smile that was almost certainly reserved for the more important visitors.

"Good afternoon, Mister Whitehead," she beamed, perfectly brilliant white teeth sparkling at him. As he looked her figure up and down, he found himself wondering if old Howard was doing her, but then she appeared too prim and proper for anything that sordid and sinful. "Will you follow me, please?" She spun on her pointed heel and headed back towards the lifts. Whitehead struggled to keep up with the pace of her long, slender, graceful legs, his eyes firmly fixed on the rear end that wriggled beneath a tight skirt like two rabbits fighting in a sack. She pressed the button for the third floor and when they exited the lift, Gil Howard was standing there, waiting for them with an annoying smile on his ruddy face.

"Glad you could make it, Roger," he said, shaking his opposite number's hand vigorously before turning to his secretary. "Thank you,

113

Jeanette. I'll be a couple of hours, I should think." She nodded imperceptibly before getting back in the lift and leaving them. Howard took him by the elbow and steered him towards the heavy wooden doors to the executive's restaurant. On entering, they were shown to a reserved table by the window overlooking the cold, grey, swirling waters of the Thames and both men sat in their respective chairs, each studying the other warily and with great care. The waiter poured two large glasses of good quality, cold Chablis before retiring to a discreet distance. The man knew better than to interrupt before he was called. Howard sipped appreciatively at the expensive wine, carefully placed the glass back on the pure white, linen tablecloth and leaned back in his padded chair, allowing his gaze to wander out of the tall windows to watch a blue and orange police motor launch as it cruised back to its station on the other side of the bridge. He wanted Whitehead to wait for a while until he was ready to speak. Let the man wonder what he had been summoned for. He knew that the wait would annoy him. The tension eventually got to Whitehead.

"Now what's all this about, Gil?" he enquired with a dismal attempt at a weak smile. "I am aware that I haven't been invited to lunch without a good reason and time is precious, you know. Besides, I have a meeting with the Prime Minister scheduled for three forty five." Howard studied the younger man sitting opposite him for a moment or two before replying.

"Don't you think it a strange coincidence that old Woolly just happened to drop dead just after the end of an operation?" he asked, sharply.

"What operation would that be, Gil? I know of no recent operations, covert or otherwise, that Lord Woolacott would have had an interest in. In fact, we've been pretty quiet of late, apart from that Diana thing, obviously."

"That's what I would have thought too. So how are you coping with all the fall-out from Operation New Broom then?" Roger Whitehead did not blink as he gazed back at the man across the table.

"New broom?" he asked quizzically. "Haven't heard of that one, old chap," he responded without a flicker. Howard threw his head back and laughed aloud, causing others in the restaurant to turn and stare. His laughter subsided a little as he leant forward and whispered conspiratorially.

"Come now, Roger," he said, "did you think your department could get away with something like that without it coming to *our* attention? Anything that happens overseas is *our* domain, you know that. You should have allowed us to assist you on this one. If you like, I can also put someone to work on finding this Hogg chappie that Gosling and your team are searching for down in the West Country."

"You mean like we could have assisted you in the matter of Lord Andrew Woolacott's unfortunate death?" Whitehead asked, his eyebrows raised. Howard inclined his head with a slight smile.

"That was all very 'last minute', old boy," he remarked. "Came down from the highest office with very little advance notice. Had to be done almost immediately, I'm afraid. By the time we had gone through all the proper channels with Section Five, it would all have been over anyway, don't you see?" Whitehead nodded slowly and tasted his wine, his mind racing ahead, trying to foresee the man's next move. It was like two chess grand masters facing off.

"You said that you might be able to do something for me, Gil?" he stated. "What was all that about?" Howard smiled and leaned ever closer to him across the starched, white linen tablecloth.

"You're not a bad chap, Roger old thing, so listen carefully to what I am about to tell you." Howard shuffled his chair closer to the table. "The P.M. himself personally gave the order for one of my operatives to take out Woolly and the intention is that once Hogg has been dealt with, *you* will be next, leaving just the P.M. and one other higher up the chain in the know." Whitehead slumped back in his high-backed chair at hearing this. Not only was he so surprised by how much Howard knew about what was going on with their current operation, but the fact that he could be killed off as easily as his predecessor almost sent him into shock. He managed, with some difficulty, to regain his composure as he leaned his elbows on the table top.

"Is this a definite, Gil? Already in the planning stage?"

"Not as far as I know at the moment, but they are banking on you clearing up this Hogg business. Once you've done that, cleared the table, so to speak, they will have no further need to keep you on, if you see what I mean. They will want to reduce the number of people who know about the operation. The possibility actually exists that I

115

may even get a directive from on high to take the P.M. out of the picture too, you never know what might happen. I have not been informed officially but I can speculate, as can you I imagine, on the original source of this directive." Whitehead paled on hearing this and sat back in his chair once again.

"And what about you, Gil?" he asked. "Who's going to deal with you?"

"No-one knows that I know anything about it," Howard replied, twirling his wedding ring on his finger. "That's how I'm in a good position to be able to help you. You and I manage to get along pretty well, …. and there's no telling who will be put into your position if you go, so I'm really looking after my own interests by tipping you the wink, so to speak." There was a long silence between the two powerful men facing each other. Eventually, Whitehead pushed his chair back and stood up, placing his napkin folded carefully on to the table.

"I appear to have lost my appetite, Gil," he said with a false smile. "Let me think this thing óver for a while and get back to you, if you don't mind. There's a lot of information to digest here." Howard looked up at him and nodded. The younger man was definitely concerned.

"Of course, old boy," he replied. "I'd expect nothing less. Don't use any of your phones though, will you. Ears everywhere, if you know what I mean. Face to face meetings would be better, I think?"

"Yes, of course. I'll be in touch." Whitehead turned for the door and then stopped and looked back. "Thanks, Gil," he said, and meant it. Howard simply nodded as he watched him leave. He turned to the waiter who had silently approached the table and stood at his elbow.

"I think I'll have the steak today, Cyril," he said, smiling up at the man.

"An excellent choice, Mister Howard, and how would you like your steak cooked sir?" Howard smiled as he answered the man.

"Just take the horns off, wipe its arse and stick it on a plate, son," he said with a huge grin. "And if it's still mooing, so much the better." Gilbert Howard liked his meat extremely rare.

* * * *

116

SOUTHEND-ON-SEA, ESSEX

OCTOBER 13TH. 1997

It was in the middle of the afternoon when Jimmy Hogg drove in to the Silver Sands Caravan Park just outside Southend town centre. He had just spent a hundred and seventy pounds on provisions from a small corner shop in one of the back streets and it was all loaded into the back seats of his hired car. The Pakistani shop-keeper must have thought that all his birthdays had come at once judging by the huge grin on his face as he rang up the purchases on his till. Seeing a small camera in the corner of the shop, Hogg had kept his head lowered although he doubted that small shops like this would have any direct link with Government sources. The caravan that he had hired for two weeks was towards the back of the park, closer to the sand dunes and, being out of season, he had no difficulty in parking right outside the plot. He wasn't too bothered about the car and had plans for it. The manager had welcomed the late visitor, especially when he paid in cash and never bothered to ask for a receipt. Hogg unloaded his shopping and stowed it all away in the spacious cupboards then went to the bathroom and shaved. Looking more like his old self, he went back outside to the hire car.

Driving within the speed limits, he arrived at the port of Harwich thirty six miles away at five fifteen. By arriving at this time, he knew the office staff would want to deal with him quickly so that they could get off home. Checking his watch, he knew he had three quarters of an hour before phoning Alan Randall as they had arranged. He parked right outside the Hertz company and went inside, twirling the keys around his finger and a well worn rucksack thrown over his left shoulder. He smiled at the iron behind the desk on the far side of the office as he got up to meet him.

"Hello there," Hogg said in his jolliest and loudest voice. He wanted to make certain that he would be remembered. "I rented this car from your Richmond office. Nice little motor. Economical too.

117

I'll need to leave it here with you as I'm catching a ferry across to Holland later on."

"Oh, I thee," lisped the ginger with a flourish of his hand. He obviously thought that his mannerisms and garish clothing, purple suit and cream shirt with an orange tie, more than made up for his speech impediment. "Have you got all your paperwork?" Hogg spread the three sheets of typed paper that he had been given on to the glass counter top. The would-be traffic-stopper scanned through them very quickly, his eyes darting across the pages, flicking his hair back with his left hand as he did so. "There ith no problem, thir," he said, turning on his heel and mincing back to his desk. "I'll jutht check the car over and then you can be on your way." Without another word, he flounced out of the office with the papers waving loosely in his hand, a heavy odour-trail of Davidoff Cool Water after shave wafting in his wake. Hogg grinned to himself and followed him into the spacious car park outside. He had noted with satisfaction the camera inside the office and another high up on the wall outside the door.

"Everything okay?" he asked at the end of the cursory inspection.

"Yeth, it ith abtholutely fine," the man replied with a smile as white as Dulux non-drip gloss paint. "What time doeth your thip thail?"

"My *what*?" Hogg asked incredulously.

"Your thip, .. your ferry?" The Doris sighed in exasperation.

"Oh, .. my *ship*. Yes, …. well a friend of mine is giving me a lift across in his refrigerated truck in a couple of hours from now." The man appeared to accept this explanation as he looked Hogg up and down. Hogg was certain that the man would remember him if questioned. The plan was that eventually, his face would be spotted on their camera and enquiries would be made at the car rental firm. They would give the information that Hogg had been planning to go across the North Sea to Holland and, hopefully, his pursuers would accept that he had left the country and there was nothing more they could do about him.

Walking back down the road in a jaunty manner, he ducked into an alleyway between two manufacturing units and tugged some clothing out of the bag, making sure that he was not being watched. He changed his pale blue jeans for crumpled black trousers and

118

swapped his light blue denim jacket for a dark green anorak with hood. In his new attire and with his head down, he set off again and it took him just over fifteen minutes to reach the main road. Time to make that call to Randall. They had both acquired new burner phones that they were certain would not have a trace on them. Making sure there were no road cameras around, he stood just round a corner and pressed the preset number. Randall answered.

"Alan, it's me," was all Hogg said.

"Are you at the place we mentioned?" Randall enquired cautiously.

"Yes, and I've done what we arranged in Harwich."

"Okay, I'll be there around four or five in the morning, the day after tomorrow. So stay inside until I get there, okay?" Randall told him. "I've arranged to borrow a friend's car as they may have tabs on mine."

"Right. I'll see you then. Oh, ..and thanks for this, Al."

"Don't worry about it, mate. We go back a long way." Randall broke the connection and tucked the mobile phone into his inside jacket pocket, looking up and down Great Windmill Street to ensure he wasn't being observed. What Randall obviously could not have known was that eyes *were* upon him from the darkened office on the second floor of an office block on the corner of Archer Street. The watcher lifted his own telephone and touched a button.

Hogg sat on his haunches in the alleyway and took out a ham sandwich wrapped in foil that he had brought along. He found he was famished and ate the snack with gusto. He wished he had had the foresight to bring a bottle of water to slake his now raging thirst. He moved up to the main road, climbed up on to the grass verge beside the road and with a great deal of hope in his heart stuck his thumb out, keeping his head lowered. After fifteen minutes he began to shiver in the cold draught from passing vehicles. Eventually, a large lorry pulled in at the kerb beside him, its air brakes hissing and the cab bouncing on its springs as it did so.

"Where you going, pal?" the driver asked, a rolled up cigarette hanging from between his lips.

"Anywhere in the direction of London will do," Hogg replied with a smile.

"Climb up then, son. I'm going right through to South London."

Heaving himself up the two steps, Hogg slumped down in the passenger seat, lowering his rucksack to the floor between his feet. The driver released the brakes and the heavy truck moved out into the traffic. Some time later, Hogg noticed a sign for Gallows Corner and the A127 trunk road to Southend.

"Can you drop me just here please, mate?" he asked the driver. "I've got a friend who lives near here and I'm hoping he'll be able to give me something to eat and a bed for the night."

"Suit yourself, mate," came the response. The driver pulled in just before the junction, causing a few horns to beep from behind. Hogg thanked him for his kindness and jumped down from the cab on to the pavement, slippery from the rain that was starting to fall in a drizzle from the dark, evening skies. He waited until the lorry had gone from sight before walking round the corner on to the dual carriageway and sticking his thumb out again. This time round he was not so lucky and stood there for over an hour before someone took pity on the bedraggled, rain-soaked figure standing forlornly beside the road and stopped. The vehicle that came to a halt beside him was an ageing, grey window cleaner's van.

"I need to get to Southend," Hogg told the young driver.

"Me too," the man replied with a grin. "Shoulda bin there 'alf an hour ago. Me missus'll go up the wall, ... *again!*" He laughed as if this state of affairs for him was a regular occurrence. Throughout the journey, Hogg had to listen to the driver's tales of housewives bedded, fiddles carried out and how much he was hen-pecked by his wife and loved to excess by his long-term mistress. Hogg simply heard the words droning into his right ear and hardly took any notice. If this wanker wanted to jabber on, then fine. He was a means to an end.

Half an hour later, in considerably heavy traffic, they pulled up by the traffic lights almost outside Southend Victoria Station. When Hogg got out, the van sped away quickly, spray spewing out from under its rear wheels. He smiled to himself, pulled his hood down over his face and walked a hundred yards back along the road. Being so dressed wouldn't arouse suspicions due to the inclement weather. He wanted to wait for a taxi to come along the road and did not want to use the rank at the station for fear of being spotted on their cameras. There was not too long to wait. Hogg asked to be dropped off at a bed and breakfast place just along from the caravan park.

The elderly taxi driver asked him about staying at a seaside B & B at this time of year, out of the usual holiday season and obviously wanted to strike up a conversation. Hogg, with his head down and face partially covered, simply mumbled yes or no to his questions.

On arrival at the faded lodging house with the once cream and pale blue paint flaking from the walls and the wooden window frames showing distinct signs of rot, Hogg paid the fare, adding a small tip and walked quickly away, leaving the cabbie muttering to himself about 'miserable bastard passengers'.

* * * *

SOHO, LONDON

OCTOBER 16TH. 1997

At three forty in the morning, two days later, Alan Randall walked away from Silk's Gentlemen's Club in Great Windmill Street leaving Rocky, the bearded barman, to close the shutters and lock up. Randall crossed over into lower Wardour Street and met a tout named Gerry outside the Wag Club. Gerry, whose all-seeing, darting eyes never missed a thing, saw Randall come round the corner by the traffic lights and smiled a welcome. He had been a tout for night clubs in Soho for many years and was a well known face. Despite his six foot two height and wide girth, Gerry was able to move quite nimbly when the need arose, for example when any plain clothes policemen entered the street. His keen eyes picked them out immediately and, as he was so conspicuous, he disappeared inside the Wag Club in an instant.

"The car's parked just down the road near the Cafe De Paris, Al," he said, fishing a set of keys from the pocket of the Crombie overcoat which he habitually wore and was his trademark. "There's almost a full tank of juice in it so make sure you fill it up when you've finished with it."

"Yeah, thanks Gerry. You want me to keep hold of it and bring it back tomorrow night?" Gerry lived in a bedsit in Poplar, East London and many miles from Randall's home in Edmonton.

"No problems," Gerry replied. "Just don't prang it, Alan. I can't afford to get another one." Randall winked at him, promising to look after the car and took the keys, walking further down the street to where the old beige Ford Cortina was parked. He found it exactly where Gerry had said. He slid behind the wheel and adjusted the driver's seat to suit his own legs. He took no notice of the young man who wandered past the car with a girl on his arm. They were just a few of the hundreds of club-goers on the street at that time. Randall had no way of knowing that the man, who had watched him leave

Silk's, was in covert radio contact with the driver of a Mitsubishi 4x4 that was coming round the corner and pulling into the kerb. Randall started the engine and, after a cursory glance in the rear view mirror, pulled out into the traffic, somewhat heavy despite the late hour but normal for Central London. The Mitsubishi merged just two cars behind him.

The number of vehicles on the road in the West End of London at that time of night was phenomenal. People on their way home in minicabs and taxis that had to contend with night buses and rickshaw cycles as well as partially inebriated pedestrians wandering across the road. Randall navigated his way through it all and headed out through Walthamstow and on to the Southend Arterial Road where the traffic had by now thinned considerably. The 4x4 vehicle tailing him had no other cars between them and dropped much further back to avoid detection. Upon reaching Southend at five twenty in the morning, Randall went North along the seafront and slightly out of the town. When he came to the metal gates of the holiday park, he stopped. The Mitsubishi had quickly pulled into the kerb two hundred yards back with its lights off and Randall never noticed it as he scanned the road behind him through his rear-view mirror. Seeing nothing untoward, he made contact with Hogg on his burner phone.

"I'm outside the gates now, Jim," he told the fugitive.

"I'll be right out in just five minutes," came the reply. As good as his word, Hogg appeared out of the gloom exactly five minutes later. He threw his holdall on to the back seat and climbed in the back, sliding down behind the front seats. The front seat passenger in the Mitsubishi saw all this through his powerful night vision binoculars and touched the driver's left arm, indicating that he should get ready to move. They had their instructions not to intervene at this point as it was only Hogg that they wanted. To have to eliminate a second person as well would give them problems that they didn't need. Observe and follow, they had been instructed. After Randall had driven back past them, they waited until the old Ford Cortina had almost got to the end of the road before starting their engine and, still with the lights switched off, making a three point turn and speeding up the road to the junction, turning left in the same direction as the Cortina. It was, however, out of sight and nowhere to be seen. The empty road stretched out ahead of them as far as they could see and the driver swore to himself, putting his foot to the floor on the accelerator in an effort to catch up with their quarry.

"Where the fuck are they?" the rear passenger asked as he leaned forward between the two front seats, his hands gripping the headrests so hard that his knuckles were turning white.

"Christ knows," the driver answered, half under his breath. "They must have gone like a bat out of hell up this road to be out of sight. They'll probably head for the main road back to London so that's what we'll make for." He dropped a gear and the engine roared as he accelerated. Randall, sitting in the driveway of a house with his lights and engine off, watched them speed past in his mirror. As he had driven away from the gates of the holiday park, although the lights of the Mitsubishi were off, his sharp eyes noticed the brake lights shine bright red as it made the three point turn in the road behind. Having turned left at the junction, he spotted the darkened driveway leading up to a garage less than a hundred yards from the junction, shielded by a small hedge and pulled straight in to it, killing the engine and lights. The occupants of the following 4x4 never noticed the parked car as their brains were telling their eyes to look for a moving car with its lights on and that is what their concentration was set on.

"Fuck me, Alan," Hogg almost sobbed from the back of the car. "That was too close for comfort, mate. What're we gonna do now?"

"Just sit tight for a few minutes in case they decide to back-track. If they don't, we'll continue as planned but in a different car."

"And exactly how do you propose to get this other car?"

"Simple. We'll park up in one of the multi-storey car parks until one of the rental offices opens at nine, then I'll go and hire one. I've got a dodgy driving licence that I always keep handy. You never know when you might need it, know what I mean?" He winked at his companion. "I'll have to use my own passport for the ferry. Takes too long to get a counterfeit one." Hogg thought this over for a moment and couldn't fault the idea. Fifteen minutes later, they were parked on the deserted fourth floor of a car park near the town centre. Hogg laid across the back seat while Randall wound down his own seat to rest his eyes. Neither of them slept really, just dozed in a half awake state, their ears aware of any noise or intrusion. At eight thirty, Randall left the car in search of a rental. After asking directions from a postman, he found the Budget Rentacar Company and it had just opened for the

124

day's business. He hired a newish Vauxhall with no problem at all, paying cash and returning to the car park. Hogg once again piled into the back of the hatchback hired car with his holdall. Randall pushed the keys into the exhaust pipe of Gerry's Cortina whilst using his burner mobile phone to call the man. He told the tout where the car and keys had been left. Gerry was not too pleased at having to get all the way to Southend to collect his old car, but understood that if Randall said that there was no option, then that was it. He knew he would be recompensed for his trouble. That's the way Alan Randall was, always looked after his mates.

By three thirty that afternoon, taking a circuitous route, Randall and Hogg had made their way to Dover and parked up near the castle to make their final arrangements. Hogg folded down one of the rear seats and crawled through to the boot. Randall then drove round to the Eastern Docks ferry terminal and approached one of the ticket booths.

"Just the day return please love," he said cheerfully to the uniformed attendant in the booth, offering his passport and the cash. "Ciggies and booze," he continued with a knowing grin. She barely glanced at him as she handed him his ticket and a piece of card to hang over his mirror showing which ferry he had been booked on to. Following her instructions, he drove round to Lane 14 and joined the queue of cars awaiting the arrival of the huge, blue and white P & O ship. Hogg crawled back through to the front of the car once more.

"Right, from here you're on your own, Jimmy my old mate," Randall told him with a smile. "I'll get out here and join the foot passengers when they get off the ferry, get on the bus and make my way out of the docks." He paused to allow the information to sink in then continued. "You simply drive the car on and drive it off when you arrive in Calais. Just wave your passport in the direction of French Customs and they always simply wave you through then you can make your way to Paris, see if you can get hold of that Frog journalist your mate Briers was talking about."

"What if the Customs stop me on the other side?" Hogg asked with a whine in his voice.

"It's a chance you'll have to take, Jim, but stand on me, I'm pretty certain you'll be alright. How are you off for money?"

"I'm holding just over a grand now, mate. I've had to shell out a shed load of dosh so far just to keep going." Randall rummaged into his inside pocket and pulled out some banknotes folded in half.

"There's a monkey there, Jim. Not a fortune but five hundred's better than a kick up the arse," he said with a smile. Hogg took the cash gratefully and stuffed it into the pocket of his anorak.

"Thanks, Al," he said. "I won't forget this."

Just then their thoughts were interrupted by the arrival of the ferry that they were due to join. They watched as it took fifteen minutes to be secured to the dock and for the ramp at the stern to be lowered. Randall levered himself from the car to allow Hogg to slide over and into the driving seat.

"Looks like we're under starter's orders, my son," he said as foot passengers started to descend to the waiting bus. "Be lucky, mate, and watch your back," was the last thing he said as he quickly weaved his way through the lines of waiting cars and boarded the bus that would take him back to the ferry terminal and the U.K. Customs desk. Once there, if asked, he would say he had been on a day trip. After the loaded bus had pulled away, a shore steward began waving cars forward to ascend the ramp and park within the bowels of the cavernous hold of the cross channel ferry. Hogg, as directed, followed the others and parked behind an old Volvo estate car. He got out, locked the door of the rental car with the remote control fob and started to climb the stairs. He was unaware of the camera that zoomed in on him as he went up. Nor did he notice another CCTV unit that followed his movements as he went along to the saloon bar close to the self service restaurant. He ordered a coffee and a small packet of biscuits from the ever open bar, taking them to a table by one of the panoramic windows. He watched with interest in the gathering darkness as hundreds of gulls flew around the ship in circles, hovering almost, waiting for any morsel of food that may be thrown to them by passengers foolish enough to be on the upper outside deck. The entire gigantic ship hummed gently to the rhythm of the idling engines as cars and articulated lorries boarded in line and he felt the vibrations through his feet as he sat at the table.

An hour and a quarter later, and twenty five minutes after its scheduled leaving time, the P & O ship was beginning to pull away from the dock and had just passed through the outer gates of Dover Docks when the captain received urgent instructions from the Coastguard high up on Langdon Cliffs. The vessel slowed to half

126

speed as the bright orange Dover Pilot's launch came alongside. The launch kept pace with the ship as three men in black boiler suits clambered across and up the ladder that had been lowered. None of the passengers on board were aware of this fact except the hardy few who were on deck for a smoke. Certainly not Jimmy Hogg who was seated at the bar now with a large gin and tonic, a croque monsieur sandwich and a carton of Silk Cut cigarettes that he had just bought.

Twenty minutes into the rough as expected channel crossing, Hogg went up the two flights of stairs and on to the open deck, unwrapping one of the packets of cigarettes from the carton as he climbed the staircase. In the shelter of the doorway to the open deck he paused and cupped his hands to light his cigarette. A middle aged couple, both in overcoats and the man wearing a cloth cap squeezed past him to make their way back downstairs and into the warmth of the saloon.

Hogg went out on to the almost empty deck, bracing himself against the cold wind that blew from the West, rocking the vessel from side to side despite the wide stabilisers just beneath the surface of the water. He steadied himself against the ship's rail as he looked out to sea. The imposing Dover Castle and the famous white cliffs were far behind him now, only just visible and he started to feel a slight sense of relief. Two young men in their early twenties were huddled against the funnel, smoking. Realising that it was probably the best place to stand with his own cigarette, in the lea of the wind, Hogg went across and stood a few feet away from them, deep in his own thoughts. The two men were discussing football results and bemoaning the fact that their team, Tottenham Hotspur, had lost an important home game, yet again. They flicked their cigarette butts over the side to disappear into the swirling, foamy water. As they started to make their way back towards the stairs, one of them nodded to Hogg.

"A bit too brisk up here for me, mate," the man said as he passed. Hogg simply smiled and nodded. None of them noticed the three shadowy figures in dark clothing lingering on the other side of the funnel. As the two football fans disappeared through the swing door, they moved stealthily forward.

* * * *

M.I.5. HEADQUARTERS

17TH. OCTOBER 1997

In his office overlooking the river, Roger Whitehead had just finished his morning coffee break whilst scanning a report on a senior Member of Parliament who had been frequenting a massage parlour-cum-brothel in his constituency to the North of London. The stupid man had let his guard down and had succumbed to some minor blackmail from a gang of small time crooks. The blackmailers, mainly youngsters had been suitably warned off and the middle-aged M.P. given advice on his future conduct regarding extra marital affairs. The coded mobile phone buzzed at his elbow as he slipped the papers back into their buff folder.

"Zulu," was all he said into the mouthpiece.

"Gosling here, Chief," came the voice. Whitehead winced perceptibly. He hated the use of that word in relation to himself. "Mission accomplished at last. The wily bastard is out of the picture for good. The job was completed yesterday, early evening. He went over the side rail of the ferry in mid channel." On hearing this, Whitehead permitted himself a huge, audible sigh of relief. The problem of James Hogg had dragged on for too long. Now it was over. There may be, he thought, another problem that needed investigation. If Hogg had been assisted by his friend Alan Randall, it was possible that the information may have been passed on. It would need looking at as a matter of some urgency.

"Well done, Gosling. It's taken you long enough to solve what should have been a very minor irritation. Get yourself back here and report to me in person. I need to know everything that has gone on in detail. Nothing is to be committed to paper or computer. Do you understand?"

"Yes, Boss. I know all about that. We'll be heading back in the helicopter within the hour and landing at Battersea Heliport."

Whitehead broke the connection and picked up the internal phone. He pressed one of the preset numbers and listened to the soft purr through the earpiece.

"Hebden here," came the gruff voice when the call was answered. Archie Hebden was the Detective Chief Superintendent at Special Branch with whom Whitehead always communicated.

"Archie, old sport," Whitehead began, "pop along and have a chat with me when you can, will you? Little bit urgent. Need to get something confirmed and one of your chaps would be ideal for what I have in mind. Shall we say two o'clock this afternoon?" There was silence for a moment before the DCI at New Scotland Yard gave his measured response. He wondered what Whitehead wanted and knew that it would not be mentioned over the telephone and so did not ask.

"Yes, …. Alright," Hebden replied, stifling a yawn. He had been to a leaving party the night before and imbibed rather more than usual of his favourite brandy. As a result, his head was pounding fit to burst. More headaches from Intelligence he did not need. "I'll come along at two."

Archibald Ronald Hebden was sixty one years old and it showed. Every year of his service was etched on his gaunt, lined face. Angular in body shape, his lower half was running to fat. A running joke was that when Hebden entered a room, his arse followed two minutes later. He had started off as a lowly police constable walking the beat in Lancashire Police and, at the age of thirty five had then transferred to the Metropolitan Police in London, hoping to find more excitement. Within a year, his abilities to sniff out crime saw him promoted to Detective Sergeant. He was then seconded to Special Branch and gradually made his way up the promotional ladder to his current position where he expected to stay until his upcoming retirement.

At the appointed hour, Hebden got out of the back of his unmarked, chauffeur driven car, wearing plain clothes despite his high rank. Going through the doors and in to the main reception of the MI5 building, he showed his Warrant Card and informed the male receptionist that Whitehead was expecting him. After a brief telephone conversation, the receptionist nodded.

"You can go straight up, Sir," he said almost begrudgingly. "I believe you know where to go?"

129

"Aye, lad, I do that," Hebden replied in his bored, Lancashire brogue, turned and headed for the bank of lifts in the far wall of the cavernous reception area. When he reached Whitehead's office, he ignored the prim looking secretary fussing over some paperwork at her desk and walked straight in to the inner office, causing Whitehead to look up from his desk with a start.

"Now then, laddie," Hebden said, hooking an upright chair out with his right foot and slumping into it, causing it to creak. "What's all this about that I have to drag myself over here?"

Whitehead gave the man a truncated version of the truth. He wanted Special Branch to make enquiries about Alan Randall to see if James Hogg had relayed any information to him at all. Hebden was given all the information that was needed on Randall, his place of work, home address and working hours. However, it had to be done with a degree of stealth so that Randall was unaware that enquiries were being made about Hogg. Archie Hebden leaned back in the chair bringing about another series of groans from the suffering wood. He clasped his hands over his paunched stomach and closed his eyes for a moment, then opened them and smiled.

"Leave it with me, Roger," he said firmly. "I'm reasonably convinced that I can get this done without difficulty. I have just the man in mind to deal with this" He pushed himself up and slowly sauntered across to the sideboard to one side of the huge window that overlooked the river and helped himself to a large measure of single malt, throwing it back in one gulp, sucking in his breath as the fiery liquid went down his throat. Anyone else would have received a rebuke from Whitehead but Archie Hebden was not a man to be trifled with. He had many friends in very high places. Fifteen minutes later, having summoned his car and driver, he was back in his own somewhat smaller office at The Yard. He picked up his private telephone and called West End Central Police Station, asking for Inspector Timothy Dixon, the S.B. Officer stationed there. He answered the call almost immediately.

"Dixon," he simply said into the instrument. Detective Inspector Timothy Jason Dixon was thirty eight years old with eleven years service within the force, three of those seconded to Special Branch. Due to his name, whilst moving up through the ranks he had been nicknamed Dixon Of Dock Green after the television police series of that name. From Sergeant onwards he was referred to simply as T.J., a name he was happy with. Life was never dull for T.J. as West End Central covered most of the West End of Central London, including the infamous Soho district where anything could, and usually did happen with alarming frequency. It also covered Oxford and Regent Streets, both rife with thieves and pickpockets. Hebden told him what was required and Dixon took it all in, making shorthand notes as he listened.

"I've got just the man for the job, Sir," he said when Hebden had eventually finished speaking. "There's a D.I. that I'm acquainted with at Vine Street nick who's well in with the Soho clubs. I believe he's earning a few quid from them. I'm sure he will know this Randall character who works on the door of the club and will probably be able to pump him for some info."

"Good, good. Get on to it as soon as you can, T.J.," Hebden responded. "Let me know how you get on, lad." He replaced the receiver and Dixon took out his personal notebook, scanning the pages at the back filled with telephone numbers and names. It didn't take him long to find the name he was searching. He called Vine Street and asked to be put through to Detective Inspector Colin Tiptree. The man was out of the office and so Dixon left a message for him to ring back as a matter of some urgency. The call was returned some thirty minutes later. He explained to Tiptree what he wanted and that the enquiries would have to be made very carefully so that no suspicions were aroused. The other D.I. said he would look into it as he knew Randall quite well. In the intervening half hour, Dixon had made some discreet enquiries and was sure that Tiptree was on the take from either Randall or his boss, or both.

That evening, Alan Randall was in his usual position in the doorway of Silk's Gentlemen's Club in Great Windmill Street, Soho. It was now just after eleven fifteen and it had so far been a quiet night. He had only made forty pounds in entrance fees when Tiptree sauntered up to him.

"Busy night, Alan?" he asked, turning up the collar of his overcoat to the chilly wind that blew the length of the road. The temperature didn't seem to bother Randall, but then he had most of his body inside the door.

"No, very slow, Colin. For a moment, I thought you might be a

131

punter. I was just about to call to you." Randall laughed at the prospect and thrust his hands deep into his trouser pockets. He looked at the D.I. with more than a little suspicion. The detective wasn't due to collect his 'wages' just yet and that was the only time he ever called round to the club. Tiptree, hunching forward and cupping his hands to light a cheroot decided to level with the man.

"Thing is, Alan my old son," he began, looking up at the doorman, "some high up faces are asking after you, wanting to know if Jimmy Hogg told you anything about a job he did in Pimlico a while back, a burglary. If he's told you anything at all, it would be better to find out now rather than later on when I wouldn't be in a position to help you out of any problems that may arise." Randall hid his despair at the question very well, although alarm bells inside his head were screaming like banshees. They must have known he had been with Hogg the day before in Southend and Dover or they wouldn't be asking questions about it now.

"Jimmy Hogg?" Randall said with a laugh. "He asked me to help get him out of the country because of some tom he had nicked that was getting too hot for him, that's all. He said that he could make his way to Amsterdam and unload the jewellery there to one of his old fences." Tiptree gazed thoughtfully at him through the blue smoke that drifted up between them from his cheroot.

"So, he's out of the country now, is he?"

"Yep. Saw him on to the ferry at Dover myself and watched it sail out. By now, if I know Jimmy, he's probably made his way to Amsterdam. The loot will be well gone by now, mate. Can't help you any further, I'm afraid, Cole." The detective nodded slowly before replying.

"Alright, Al. I'll pass all that on, let them know he's had it away on his toes and travelled to foreign climes." With that, he gave Randall a half wink, turned and made his way back towards Piccadilly Circus. When he reached his office he took out the mobile number that T. J. Dixon had given him to call with any results, at any time, day or night. The Special Branch man thanked him for his trouble and made a call of his own, relaying the information to Hebden who in turn passed it to Roger Whitehead at MI5. Whitehead received the information with a degree of satisfaction. Had Randall been better informed, there was no doubt that

132

Whitehead would have had him silenced permanently. This just meant that they did not have the problem of having to remove another body from the operation. Whitehead sat back and smiled warmly to himself.

* * * *

WESTMINSTER, LONDON

19th OCTOBER 1997

Despite being late Autumn, it was a relatively warm, sunny afternoon as Jonathan Wycke left No.10 Downing Street by the rear entrance once more. He had been summoned by the Prime Minister for yet another special covert operation. Bearing in mind what had been happening over recent months, he was not at all surprised at the intended target this time. He returned to the MI6 Headquarters and went immediately up to the top floor to bring his chief, Gilbert Howard, up to date. The man's secretary, Jeanette, glanced up over her heavy, horn-rimmed glasses as Wycke emerged from the lift. He flashed one of his smiles at her which she returned. Despite being a couple of years older than this man, she had always secretly fantasised about him, yearning for his touch, imagining what it would be like to be held by those strong, muscular arms, feeling his naked flesh against hers. Her breasts heaved slightly before she spoke.

"You can go straight in, Sir," she said with a broad smile, depressing a small button on her desk so that the door to the great man's office buzzed quietly. "He's been expecting you for some time." Wycke knew the woman's weakness and lowered one eyelid ever so slightly in a half wink.

"Thank you, Jeanette," he said and went through. Whenever he gave her that look, she almost felt faint and a warm glow overcame her entire body, causing her to shudder a little. She watched his broad back as he went through the doorway and disappeared from view. She continued to stare as the door hissed slowly shut behind him and sighed to herself. 'If only'.

Wycke nodded at his superior as he entered.

"Ah, Jonathan," Gilbert said, ushering him to a seat beside his desk. "What has the P.M. got up his sleeve now?" Wycke adjusted the cuffs of his shirt that protruded from the sleeves of his Saville Row suit before he replied.

"It's Roger Whitehead this time, Sir," he told the man. "I had been expecting something like this ever since that business with Lord Woolacott. There's something going on there at Section Five and I'm convinced that it has something to do with the events in Paris a short while ago. However, I am being told nothing, I am just surmising. I believe that Whitehead may just be the last person in the chain who knows anything, apart from the Prime Minister himself, of course." Gilbert sat back in his seat as he listened and took in all this information. He felt sure that Wycke was right, after all he was no fool, and Gilbert also had suspicions himself. He had heard rumours of Operation New Broom and, reading between the lines and listening to exchanges, had an inkling of the operation's purpose and where it had originated. He pushed his glasses up his rounded nose, his brows knitted together in a serious frown. He sat like that for almost a minute, his brain working in overdrive like a well oiled machine.

"Okay, Jonathan," he said at length. "I'll leave it to you to make all the necessary arrangements and plans. Let me know if I can help in any way at all but, as before, this is all off the record and nothing to do with this department. There must be no comebacks whatsoever."

"I understand that, Sir. I am informed by the Premier that things must be brought to a satisfactory conclusion very swiftly, so I shall have to make haste with the planning which will, of necessity, have to be meticulous."

"Of course. I'll leave everything in your capable hands, my boy, You have carte blanche at all levels within the department." Gilbert told him with a confident nod of his balding head so that the spectacles began to slide back down. Wycke left the man's office, his mind turning over various possibilities. So pre-occupied in thought was he that he didn't even glance in Jeanette's direction as he passed her desk on his way to the lift. She smiled, hoping that he would turn, see her and return the smile. He did not. The lift arrived with a 'ding', he entered and was gone.

Back in his own smaller office, he poured coffee from the percolator that steamed on the top of a filing cabinet, sat in his comfortable armchair near the window and started to put together some sort of plan of action.

Three days later, Roger Whitehead left his gated detached four bedroomed, two bathroomed house set in its own grounds on Tyler's Causeway just outside Newgate Street Village in Hertfordshire. He drove his Daimler into the town of Cuffley and pulled in to a Gulf service station. It was seven fifteen and he had suffered a late night with drinks at Whitewebbs Golf Club until well gone midnight. With his head fuzzy, he wished he could have shied away from the office that day but outstanding work pressures meant that his absence would cause problems. He yawned as he reached for the nozzle of the petrol pump. It was at that precise moment that a small Renault Clio drove up on the opposite side of the pump. The heavily bearded driver, wearing traditional Arab clothing, skull-cap and sandals jumped out, pulling a large handgun from beneath his flowing robes. He aimed the gun at Whitehead and started shouting in a loud voice as Whitehead reached for his own holstered gun.

"*Allahu akbar!, ... Allahu akbar!*" The un-silenced pistol fired twice, loudly, the heavy gauge bullets hitting Whitehead in the front and side of his skull, sending him sprawling across the boot of his own car and to fall on his back behind it, his arms spread out, palms upwards as if in crucifixion. A middle-aged woman doctor refuelling her Volkswagen screamed and ducked for cover, fear etched on her ashen face. The gunman then turned and fired two more shots towards the forecourt shop, shattering the glass door and one of the windows, before turning back to the man on the ground. He put another shot into the already dead man's forehead then calmly walked to his own vehicle. He got in, the engine still running, and pulled gently away before accelerating around to the left at the top of the hill.

A quarter of a mile further on, the bearded man turned his car into a gate that led through some trees and to a field where he parked behind another hedgerow. He got out and retrieved a can of petrol from where he had left it earlier beside a tree. Having poured the contents liberally around the interior of the Renault, he carefully removed the false beard that had been held expertly in place with spirit gum, the Arab clothing and sandals and threw them inside the car, along with the rubber gloves he had been wearing since collecting the car, leaving the door open. He went across to the hedge and pulled away some branches to reveal a Honda 125 motorcycle, a crash helmet and leather jacket dangling from the handlebars. The gunman donned the jacket and helmet, started the machine and rode slowly over to the open door of the car. The high explosive timer grenade he placed on the seat of the car before closing the door would give him sixty seconds to get clear. The rider had turned on to the main road towards Enfield and was two hundred yards away before the explosion ripped through the old car. The sound could be heard even through his crash helmet and Jonathan Wycke smiled to himself in satisfaction as he twisted the throttle to increase speed.

Later that afternoon, having returned home to shower and change, Wycke went in to Howard's office. The head of MI6 looked up at him inquisitively. Wycke simply nodded as he sat down.

"Everything went as expected, Sir," he said. "I feel certain that the subterfuge worked perfectly." He was right. On the television news bulletins that evening and on headlines in the following day's papers the horrific daylight assassination of the Director of MI5 was, as was the desired intent, laid firmly on the shoulders of Muslim radical fundamentalists.

When Wycke had left Gilbert's office, his secretary Jeanette had her back to him and was bending over a filing cabinet. Wycke stopped and coughed politely. She stood up and turned sharply. Seeing it was him, she smiled sweetly and smoothed her skirt as she approached her own desk.

"Is there anything I can help you with, Sir?" she asked. Wycke had been having a lean time of late with the opposite sex and decided that period should come to an end at the earliest opportunity.

"Yes, Jeanette," he said, sitting on the edge of her desk. "You can join me for dinner this evening; that would be a big help. I very much need to unwind a little." She caught her breath, hardly daring to believe he was asking her.

"Yes," she replied without hesitation. "I'd love to, if you're sure it's not against any protocol?"

"I'm reasonably certain that it's not. Jot down your address and I'll pick you up. Shall we say seven thirty?"

"That would be lovely," she responded with a tremor in her voice as she frantically scribbled down her address on the notepad she kept beside her computer screen, her hand shaking ever so slightly. He took the slip of paper that she handed him, folded it and slid it into his top pocket.

"I'll see you later, then." With that, he levered himself off of her desk and went to the lift. As he pressed the button to call it, he turned, smiled, gave a wink and then went into the lift as it arrived.

At seven thirty five, Wycke rang the bell for Jeanette's flat near Clapham Junction. She answered the door almost as if she had been standing right behind it. With her hair brushed down, she looked quite stunning, he thought. The evening was beginning to look as if it had been an excellent idea after all. She pulled the door closed behind her and hooked her arm through his. When they reached the street, Wycke put his arm up and a taxi pulled in as if by magic. They dined well at Polgati's Italian Ristorante in Battersea, an area South of the river that had once been run down but was now becoming quite fashionable. Having finished off a bottle and a half of very pleasant Pinot Grigio, they left at ten forty. As they went out through the door, another taxi stopped to allow passengers to alight. Wycke quickly grabbed the open door and ushered Jeanette inside. Another example of the magic that this wonderful man possessed, she thought, settling back in the seat. When they reached her flat some fifteen minutes later, Wycke paid off the driver with a handsome tip and followed her up the staircase to her front door. She put the key into the lock then turned to look at him. She was unsure of what to say but he took control of the situation by speaking first.

"I must warn you, Jeanette," he started with a disarming smile, "that if you invite me inside, I can not guarantee to leave before morning." His questioning gaze left no doubt as to his meaning.

"In that case, you had better come in," she replied, opening the door wide and going through. He followed her inside the flat and within minutes they were both naked on her large double bed. They made love twice. First hard and fast and then again, twenty minutes later. This time more leisurely, much slower and loving. She had never experienced multiple orgasms before but then she thought she had never been so much in love with a man like this before either. They eventually fell asleep, exhausted, in each other's arms at around four in the morning. Her dreams were filled with images of Jonathan

Wycke above her, his smiling face gazing down at her as he thrust himself inside her. When she awoke to her automatic alarm clock at six thirty, he was gone. Wrapping a robe around herself, she went through to the kitchen to find a note propped up on the table. It was simply marked with a large 'X' in her own red lipstick.

* * * *

BUCKINGHAMSHIRE GOLF CLUB

29TH. OCTOBER 1997

The earlier rain that had threatened to ruin the ceremony to open the new club house had dissipated first to a fine drizzle and had now stopped altogether. The smell of fresh rain on recently mowed grass filtered through the large, open wooden doors to the assembled dignitaries and club members as they waited patiently for their honoured guest to arrive and officially open the newly refurbished building. The somewhat comforting smell of nature gradually mingled with that of fresh paint and varnish the further inside one went. It was a good course with enough rough patches to make the eighteen holes something of a challenge.

At exactly one fifteen, as arranged, the helicopter hove into view from the south-east, hovered above the first green for a moment and then moved slightly before turning a full one hundred and eighty degrees to face the wind before gently descending on to the eighteenth green. As the enormous rotors slowed, the door opened and a small stair case was lowered from the fuselage. The Prime Minister made his way gingerly down the steps and was greeted by the Chairman of the club, shaking his outstretched hand vigorously. After a brief conversation punctuated with smiles and laughter, the two men and their entourage walked across the closely cropped grass and disappeared from view inside the clubhouse.

Jonathan Wycke, wearing a camouflaged jump-suit and balaclava, had watched all this through the Leupold Mk 4 telescopic sight of his Remington M-24 sniper rifle. He made a slight adjustment to the sights and resumed his pose, lying flat in wet grass beneath the bushes two hundred yards distant on the other side of the Colne River, waiting patiently for the right moment. His unmoving prostrate figure blended perfectly into the surroundings. A walker could possibly have passed within a few feet without noticing him. So still was he that a wood louse crept across his arm without any fear. The grey rain clouds began at last to diminish and sunshine streamed down on the lush, green fields, and sparkled on the ripples of the slow moving river like diamonds cast upon a deep blue-green velvet cloth.

After an hour and ten minutes, exactly as expected, the head of Her Majesty's Government came out of the building surrounded by his security men and a few of the upper echelons of the golf club. Among them was one of the more long-standing members, Paul Gosling, wearing his blue blazer sporting the emblem of the club on his breast pocket. He was all smiles as he shook hands with the Prime Minister before the man went up the steps and back on board the helicopter for the journey back to Central London. Gosling, along with the other members moved away from the aircraft as its engines started and the huge blades above it started to rotate. The noise was deafening as the machine lifted slowly from the ground. It was at this point, when the engine sound and vibration was at its highest that Wycke pulled gently on the trigger. The bullet hit Gosling just below his right eye and knocked him from his feet, almost in a cartwheel to send him sprawling to the ground. Travelling at a mean speed of 2,580 feet per second, the 175 grain, hollow point bullet had exploded after entering the victim's head, taking out the left side of his cheek and ear as well, sending blood spattering everywhere. As the shot had been drowned out by the engine noise, it took a few moments to register on the other spectators that something was very wrong.

From the side window of the giant helicopter, the Prime Minister dispassionately watched all this and turned away, looking down at some paperwork. Yet another problem had been dealt with.

As Gosling hit the ground, Wycke was up and running, crouched beneath the tops of hedges. As he ran, he folded his sniper rifle in to the bag that he had slung across his shoulders. He reached the tow-path beside the Grand Union Canal only three minutes after taking the shot. This was where his Honda motorcycle was expertly hidden in the bushes, covered with snapped off branches. Wycke straddled the machine and put on the full-face helmet that he had left on the handlebars, switched on the engine and set off in a southerly direction, keeping the revs low. After a few minutes, having slowed considerably whilst weaving between dog walkers and the like, he crossed a narrow bridge that took him to the opposite side of the canal and then stopped in a tunnel that passed beneath Western Avenue, the main dual carriageway A40 trunk road in to London. With a push, the Honda motorbike went quickly into the water and disappeared from view within seconds. Wycke scrambled up the embankment and reached the road then walked the hundred yards to the lay-by where he had previously parked an old Ford Escort. The vehicle had been stolen the night before and had the registration plates changed to an identical car. Wycke had left a large note in the windscreen notifying anyone who looked that he had broken down and gone for assistance.

Driving within the speed limit, he reached the turn off for White City some fifteen minutes later, continuing past the BBC Centre and parking the car in Bulwer Road. Retrieving a small holdall from the passenger foot well and with the rifle bag over his shoulder, a short walk brought him to the busy Shepherds Bush Green where he found a public convenience block. Wycke went down the litter-strewn steps and locked himself into one of the vacant cubicles. From the holdall he removed a rolled up, thin, blue raincoat and a pair of well worn trousers. His camouflage outfit went inside the bag with the gloves he had been wearing and he zipped it closed. Wearing the other set of clothes and a pair of heavy rimmed fake spectacles, he walked out of the toilets looking completely different. Within minutes, he was in the back of a black cab and being whisked along to Vauxhall and the MI6 Building.

On entering the echoing, cavernous hall of the fortified building, he went straight to the sub-basement area and, using his ID card to swipe entry, went through a huge metal doorway. A well-built, armed, uniformed security guard stood up abruptly and faced him as he entered.

"Afternoon, Mister Wycke," he said with a warm smile that belied the thoroughness of his position. He would shoot a man as soon as look at him. "Don't often see you down here, sir. What can we do for you?"

"Just a few articles to be disposed of, Daniel," Wycke replied, raising the gun bag and holdall slightly.

"Very good, sir," he replied, eyeing the two bags. "I'll get Mister Rowbotham to take them off you." With that, he lifted a telephone from the desk and made a call, speaking quietly into the receiver. Less than a minute later, Michael Rowbotham came through a side door.

"Hello, Jonathan," he began. "What have you got for me now?" He approached and looked down at the two bags the other man was carrying.

"Just a bit of clothing, a motorcycle crash helmet and a pair of gloves," he replied and then, almost as an afterthought added, "Oh, and a used weapon as well." At this point he allowed a slight smile to etch its way into the corners of his mouth. Rowbotham was well aware of Wycke's deadly purpose within the department and took both the bags without question.

"Leave it all with me, Jonathan," Rowbotham responded, taking both bags. He went back through the door and Wycke turned away, leaving the room by the same way he had entered.

"Have a good day, Mister Wycke," said Daniel, the security guard as he left.

* * * *

SOHO, LONDON

14th. DECEMBER 1997

At two forty five in the morning, Great Windmill Street was quiet, cold, damp and, as most of the neon lights had been extinguished for the night, looking very dismal indeed. There was a sheen on the road and pavements from the showers that had been falling every now and then throughout the night. Alan Randall had been standing in the doorway of Silk's Gentleman's Club since just before eight o'clock the previous evening. Seven bastard hours, he was thinking to himself, and only two lousy, penny-pinching punters in the place all night. Twenty five pounds was all he had managed to take. Yet another bad night. Times were getting harder. In the distance on the opposite side of the road he noticed Joe the Malt come out of his strip show and begin to wind up the bright orange canvass awning that covered the entrance to the seedy joint. Pissy Chris, one of the regular touts, walked forlornly in a shuffling motion towards him from the lower end of the street and stopped beside the door.

"You done any good tonight, Alan?" he asked, looking completely miserable and down at heel.

"No, mate," he replied with a slow shake of his head and stuffing his now chilled hands into his trouser pockets. "Only two customers all night. I tell you, Chris, it's getting worse. If things carry on like this, I might even have to go and get myself a proper job. And that's not as easy as it sounds."

"Fuck me! It *must* be bad," he responded with a chortle and wandered off into the night.

Randall watched his back disappear in the distance then sniffed, looked up and down the street for a moment and flicked his cigarette butt out into the roadway to land with a small shower of red sparks like a miniature firework display. Only another quarter of an hour or so then it would be time to pull down the shutters and go home. He was looking forward to getting in to his little flat and kicking his

144

shoes off before dropping on to his king sized bed. Just a shame there was no-one to share it with him tonight, he thought. He briefly considered one of the hostesses who had been giving him the glad eye of late but then dismissed the idea. He'd only have to give her breakfast and drive her home the next morning.

A couple of middle-aged businessmen in dark overcoats wandered down from the top end of the street. Randall waited until they almost drew level with him and then stepped out of the doorway.

"Yes, gentlemen," he said with a beaming smile which belied the way he was actually feeling. "You've come to just the right place. Looking for a late night drink? A couple of girls, maybe? This is the best place in town for both if you fancy it. Only ten pounds each to get in."

"No thank you, young man," one of them, the taller of the pair replied with a hint of a sneer through half closed eyes behind rimless glasses. "We know all about these kind of places. We've already been fleeced out of too much money once tonight, thank you." With their noses pointed skyward, they continued their journey down the road towards Piccadilly Circus. Randall watched them go and knew that was the last chance he was likely to get that night.

"Wankers!" he muttered to himself. A gruff voice called out from behind the multi-coloured beaded curtain that led to the bar.

"Alan! Telephone for you."

"Okay, Rocky," he responded with a sigh. "On my way." He sauntered into the tiny bar area and took the telephone receiver that the bearded barman was holding out, wondering who the hell would be calling him there at this time of the night. "Cheers, Rock." Taking the instrument he spoke into the mouthpiece. "Hello?" There was total silence on the line for a few moments and then came a voice he knew well that caused him to hold his breath.

"Alan? …. You know who this is, don't you?" Randall knew in an instant but cautiously hid his surprise from the barman and Cindy, the hostess who had been hovering in the bar for most of the evening. It was his old friend Jimmy Hogg. There was no mistaking the voice.

"How are you doing, mate?" he asked, genuinely pleased to hear from his old partner in crime.

"I'm doing great, Al."

"What happened after I left you?" He was interested to find out

145

where his old friend had been hiding out. "From what I heard from our local tame copper, you went over the side of the ferry."

"Someone did, but not me." Hogg said with a slight chuckle. He went on to recount the events of that night. "I was sitting on the deck in the dark with my back to the funnel, having a cigarette when I saw these three blokes dressed in black overalls approach some geezer who was standing by the rail, looking out to sea. They just grabbed him by the legs and tipped him overboard in less than two seconds. When I saw what was happening, I slid underneath one of the benches on the deck and kept quiet until they left. I stayed there until we docked."

"Jesus! So an innocent party got mistaken for you, it seems.!

"Looks that way." There was a pause and Randall heard the rasp of a cigarette lighter as Hogg flicked it with his thumb. "Anyway, I kept well out of sight until the ferry docked in Calais then got back into the car and simply drove off and out of the docks. No-one even looked at me. It really was that easy." Randall smiled to himself as he imagined Jimmy's face when he drove through the French Customs gate.

"So what have you been doing for the past couple of months?"

"Got myself a nice little labouring job with some builders in Coulomby, a little village just outside Saint-Omer. It's all cash in hand so no paperwork needed. I'm renting a room above the boulangerie, a baker's shop in Coulomby. Learned quite a bit of French as well. Had to, d'you see?" He heard Hogg take a deep drag on his cigarette before he continued his story. "Had to get used to these bloody French cigarettes as well. They're fucking strong, mate, I can tell you. Almost blow your bastard head off. You wouldn't recognise me now, Al. No-one would. I've grown a big, bushy beard and shaved all my hair off."

"Where are you phoning from, Jim?"

"I've bought myself a cheap burner phone from the big Auchan store in Saint-Omer. Untraceable."

"Well don't give me the number, Jimmy. After Christmas when I've got a week or so off, I might drive over and see you, catch up a bit, you know? It's only about a thirty minute drive from the Channel Tunnel and I'm sure I can find the baker's shop if, as you say, it's a small village, eh?"

"Yeah, that'd be great, Alan. Bring some decent cigarettes will you? Oh, and some decent tea bags. The stuff you get here tastes like shite." Hogg sounded as pleased as punch to hear Randall's suggestion. "Be nice to be able to speak to someone properly instead of having to shout and make hand gestures to get yourself understood. I'm sure these bloody Frogs understand more English than they let on. They just want to be bloody-minded." Randall laughed along with him

"You're probably right, Jim," he told him. I reckon they still haven't forgiven us for Agincourt."

"Ashen what?"

"Doesn't matter, Jimmy," Randall laughed aloud. "I'll see you in a few short weeks, mate."

"Alright, Al," Hogg replied. I'll look forward to it." With that, he ended the call, leaving Randall looking at the handset in wonder. He thought he had seen the last of Jimmy Hogg.

About two miles away as the crow flies, in the MI6 building at Vauxhall, a man switched off the telephone recording machine he had been glued to through every shift for the past couple of months, took off his headphones and lifted the internal phone to call the top floor office of the top man, Gilbert Howard.

* * * *

THE END.

147

L - #0128 - 250621 - C0 - 210/148/9 - PB - DID3116008